A LOW COUNTRY
#CityOfSnakes

Thanks for your support

Sherman

Sherman T. Smalls

Copyright © 2019 by **Sherman T. Smalls**

Cover Design by A. Anita/ Designer_pro247

Connect with the Author:
Email: Stsmalls32@yahoo.com
Facebook: Sherman T. Smalls
Instagram: Dr Cools_101
ISBN: 978-1-5136-4883-5

DEDICATION

This is a testament for every male and female dedicated to life change not only for themselves but also for the people they adore.

TABLE OF CONTENTS

ACKNOWLEDGMENTS vii

CHAPTER 1 1

Pilot **1**

CHAPTER 2..23

The Hunt...**23**

CHAPTER 3..40

A Hard Life..**40**

CHAPTER 4..63

The Mule **63**

CHAPTER 5..86

The Basement **86**

CHAPTER 6..98

Deception **98**

CHAPTER 7..112

The Plot...**112**

CHAPTER 8..129

The Breakdown **129**

CHAPTER 9 151

   Heartless **151**

CHAPTER 10...171

   Lost..**171**

CHAPTER 11 187

   New Beginnings **187**

CHAPTER 12...209

   Last Laugh..**209**

CHAPTER 13...223

   City of Snakes **223**

CHAPTER 14...237

   Exposed **237**

CHAPTER 15...259

   Tammy's Revenge **259**

CHAPTER 16...287

   The Breakthrough **287**

   ABOUT THE AUTHOR...............................**298**

ACKNOWLEDGMENTS

I would like to first acknowledge my Father, The Most High, for blessing me with this incredible gift to share with everyone around the world; without Him none of this would have been possible. I would also like to thank Aida Chenevieve Emanuels, Tammy Washington, Sonya Johnson, Candis Dateisha Watts, Ashly Kee, and Editor_pro10 from Fiverr for the amazing job they've done with editing my book. I would also like to acknowledge A. Anita/ Designer_pro247 from Fiverr for an amazing book cover and Fernando Henry Z. from Freelancer for a job well done with a kickass short video. Lastly, I want to give a special thanks to my family for giving me the strength to push forward and complete my book. Without you guys' inspiration, I would have never made it this far.

CHAPTER 1
Pilot

*I*t was 1996, heavy drops of rain fell on the football field as the crowd roared back at the sight of their star quarterback being carried from the muddy terrain, with his hands in the air, prideful. It was the first time Columbia High had won State in fifteen years, thanks to James Jones. It was his last year in high school, and he could feel the piercing eyes of the scouts watching him from the sideline.

James was tall, slim, with a powerful arm and relentless speed. Just the sight of him made the team appear professional. His two best friends, Crazy Cory, who played tight end, and Killa Man, who played defensive tackle, were almost as skilled as he was, and together they went on to win one of the biggest games of their high school career. Both Crazy Cory and Killa Man were big guys. The average person would think they were well beyond their age. They both wore full-grown men beards, with hard faces. The mischief they caused in school far exceeded their grade point averages, but the whole school loved them, even the teachers and staff. Everywhere they went in the city; people knew their names. They were definitely considered the "celebrities" of their community. But, their celebrity status only went so far. All three players knew they shared one common ground; they were all still broke, after each game, and no one cared if they had a hot meal. As long as they kept winning games, they were "heroes," but their real fight wasn't on the football field, it was in their homes. Both James and Killa Man's mothers were on crack. And for Cory's mom, everyone knew she was a compulsive alcoholic, who verbally and physically abused him. Although Cory had much more to endure at home, he still had one thing his other friends didn't have, an outlet. He worked with his uncle and cousin; helping them build a small diner. Despite their similar differences, their bond was on the football field. That's where they displayed their anger and rage and consistently focused on crushing their opponents.

The three young men walked the sidewalk, still amped up from the game over the weekend; Killa Man could hear his stomach twirl with a heavy growl.

"Man! I'm hungry, how much money you got, James?!" said Killa Man with his hands clenching his stomach, still sore from the game.

Killa Man got his name from the insane, beast type style he showed on the football field and he was just as intense when it came to throwing a punch. Both of the friends continued to ignore the two hundred and fifty-pound hungry senior, Killa Man slightly punched James on the arm as he repeated his question, "Nigga, you got some money?!"

"Naw bro! Shit, do you have some money?" James asked with an annoying frown.

He had just lost his last few dollars shooting dice in the school bathroom and would be broke until he could hustle some more cash. People closest to him knew of his situation and helped him out; giving him odd jobs here and there, like cutting grass or painting. The money wasn't enough to live on, but at least it helped put some food on the table for him and his siblings.

"Nigga, we don't need no money. You know my uncle just opened Cora's Diner on the corner of Main Street. Plus, my cousin works there…", stated Crazy Cory, and before he could get another word out, James and Killa Man simultaneously said, "Grace!" as they both imagined a vivid picture of the sexy senior.

"Hell yeah!" I'm all, with it!" said James smiling, rubbing his palms together and licking his lips while drawing a picture of Grace in his mind. He thought of how fine she was with her light-skinned complexion, emerald green eyes, slim trimmed waist, and not to mention, a real plump ass to match her sexy figure. James and Grace knew each other since they were kids. They both held a secret crush but were too shy to take the first step; casually flirting, every chance they got. Finally, they arrived at Cora's Diner with empty pockets and growling stomachs.

Grace and her father decided to name the Diner "Cora's Diner," in loving memory of her deceased mother. The aroma of hamburgers and fries spiked their noses as the boys entered. James and Killa Man were amazed at the setup, as they walked through the beautiful establishment.

Chuckling, Killa Man pointed towards Cory and said jokingly, "Ay, man! Look, we got Cory the carpenter in this muthafucka," as he laughed, still admiring the small but very fancy Diner.

Noticing no one found his joke funny, Killa Man continued, with a more serious tone, "I'm just kidding, you and your "fam" really did y'all thing," he said humbly, reaching out to give Cory a dap on a job well done.

Most of the customers greeted them with friendly smiles while patting them on the back and congratulating them on their success. All three graciously smiled, accepting their homage. As they scrolled through the Diner, before reaching the front counter, Killa Man bulldozed his way in front of Cory and James to ensure he was the first one in front of Grace. He leaned on the end of the marble countertop and said, "Aye sexy... tell me something good?" with a silly smirk on his face.

Staring at Killa Man, Grace rolled her dazzling green eyes, then, with a flirtatious smile turned to James and asked about his day, batting her beautiful emerald greens, as she gazed in his eyes.

Grace liked James as much as he liked her, but she did all she could to not give in to his temptations. She respected and protected her father's feelings. She was the only thing he had left. After her mom died from cancer, a few years ago, her father took the leftover insurance money and pursued his dreams of owning a business. The Diner became a major priority to her, and she was determined to help her dad run it successfully before she had to leave for college.

As James caught her gaze, he replied, "My day is perfect now," in a cool smooth demeanor and stared at her as if it was his first time seeing her. He gave Grace a warm smile, then walked around the counter to embrace her with a bear hug. James always enjoyed moments like these, lifting her from her feet, while smelling her peachy scented skin. As he slowly let go of her waist, he said jokingly "I like your new threads," referring to the "chef-like" outfit her father made her wear. "And... I like what y'all done with this place too. I'm surprised you guys got anything done with Crazy helping you," James said, acknowledging Cory's playful ways.

"He did alright, he worked... but, he also ate half the profit," Grace said jokingly.

"Ok! Ok!" Crazy Cory loudly expressed, interrupting the conversation.

Don't you think you comedians had enough of the Cory show? But, since we are on the subject of eating?" Cory said while rubbing his stomach. "Ask Unc".

"Ask Unc what?" said Mo, responding with a deep voice that seemed to draw the attention of customers in the Diner and clearly affecting the loud chatter.

All three, once confident young men, suddenly lost their words at the sight of Grace's father approaching them from the kitchen. Mo was old school and had a no-nonsense approach. The guys respected him for the wisdom he shared and the knowledge he gave them, every time they came around. He was the father figure none of them had, and all of them wish they had.

Before Cory could respond, Mo said, "I saw the game over the weekend… I tell you… you guys play a helluva game! Your meal is on the house today." Mo smiled, showing his one gold tooth in the front of his mouth. He continued to walk past each of the young men, congratulating them while patting James on the shoulder.

The trio responded simultaneously and said, "Thanks!" with hungry smiles, watching as Mo pushed through the swinging double doors leading to the kitchen to prepare their meals.

James focused all his attention back on Grace as she smiled and said sarcastically, "You guys look like you could use a bite to eat... plus after the big win Friday, I think y'all deserve it."

The guys looked at each other and smiled, feeling like royalty.

She greeted her cousin Crazy Cory with a warm smile and a strong country accent and asked, "And where have you been the last two weeks, Cory? It's starting to pick up, and we could really use your help."

You could tell that Cory was thinking hard to respond with a lie, but could not think of one, and simply ignored her question. Noticing she would never get an honest reply, she walked away with an attitude.

"Damn man, you ain't been to work in two weeks, is everything ok, bro?" James asked while admiring Grace's curves as she walked towards the kitchen.

Crazy Cory sighed and insisted that everything was okay. But, they both knew he was lying. His mom would get sloppy drunk, most nights, and cuss the inspiration out of him. They all believed the main reason why his uncle Mo gave him a job was to keep him motivated and out of trouble. If it weren't for football and the support of his team, Cory might have ended up another lost soul.

Changing the subject, Killa Man cut some of the tension in the air and said, "Man, you crazy if you ain't hit that yet, James!! She fine as hell and she gives free food, Nigga! She feeding you already!" James glared at Killa Man and said with all confidence, while he shook his head in agreement, "Yeah, you right!"

"Nigga! That's my damn cousin!!! You two horny bastards talking about, plus Grace ain't giving up no pussy to none of y'all fools!! No way. My uncle would kill her ass," an overprotective Crazy Cory said as he stood up, putting James in a headlock, knowing he had a crush on her for years.

Big walked in the small Fast Food Diner, with his entourage behind him, talking loud and being unruly. A strong scent of weed reeked in their clothes, as they strolled the dining room floor, spiking the nose of the customers they passed. As Big and his crew approached the three teens, he put his hand on James's shoulder.

The diamonds in Big's Rolex sparkled like the colors of the rainbow. His gold rope twinkled to his slightest movement. His clothes were neat, and his pants sharply creased. His facial features were sturdy, scarred with wounds from street wars.

He said, "Hey cuz what's up?" while staring at Cory watching him undress the tall, dark stallion that stood next to him, with his eyes.

"Ay, Lil nigga... you have seen her a million times before, pick up your lip!" Big said jokingly to Cory, watching him snap out of his hypnotic state.

Big continued, "I watched the game over the weekend. Y'all Lil niggas were out there. Whipping ass and taking names," he said nobly looking down at James.

Big patted James on the shoulder and said, "This boy right here got an arm on him. I like this guy."

James looked over his shoulder, only to peer in Big's cold eyes.

"Preciate it, man," he said, trying to brush off the crazed drug dealer as he turned back to face his friends.

Ignoring James's suggestion to leave him and his friends alone, Big said, "Come here, bruh… I wanna holler at you, for a second."

Not having any idea what the "kingpin" of the city could possibly want with him, James stared at his friends in anguish, feeling his heart beating from his chest, not from fear, but with anticipation of what Big could possibly want. Big put his arm over James's neck, leading him to the back of the fast-food joint.

Big was the "kingpin" of his city. Even though he didn't stay anywhere near the neighborhoods he corrupted, he kept his ears to the ground so he would never lose his connection with the streets. There wasn't a corner in Columbia that had not tasted his dope. He certainly lived flamboyantly. He was the proud owner of a ten-bedroom house in the suburbs, with a swimming pool and a few old school Chevys, along with a couple of luxury cars, to match his lavish lifestyle. Everyone knew Big had a shit load of drugs and lots of money. He also had connections and managed to keep himself out of the spotlight. Cops, along with politicians, turned a blind eye to the evil he unleashed on these communities.

Murder and crime were at an all-time high, and there wasn't a dead body in the streets he didn't know about. He flooded the streets with dope, and a lot of people ate well. The streets feared him, and the ladies loved him. His muscles were Joey and Josh. They never touched the cash or dope; their job was to make sure the money was on time and never short. And of course, snitches came up either missing, dead in the streets, or left somewhere in horrible shape.

Big stayed two steps ahead of the game. He had a loyal and intelligent woman named Tammy. A tall, dark, thick, classy chick that didn't fit the profile of a rich drug dealer. But, she gave a very shady vibe, like the rest of the guys in his crew. The only difference was, her immaculate beauty covered her treacherous heart. Big met Tammy a few years ago when she was fresh out of college. She was a struggling, single parent of one, and became the heart of his operation. She never saw the product, just the money, but directed the flow of both.

Big was smart! He would often switch the stash houses to throw his workers and the police off. Tammy would give orders to the workers, to switch houses, roughly every three months. But, there was one thing that never changed: her drops of cash. Tammy's routine was to drop blocks of cash in a black duffle bag, twice a month, to a vacant black truck. The truck was always in the same parking spot every Friday night, after the football games. Even during the offseason, the spot never changed. Big never let anyone see his product, handle his money, or connect with his people all at the same time. That was his way of protecting himself. He figured, the more a person knew, the more dangerous that person could become. Being heavy in the dope game, he just thought everyone was counting his money in their devious minds and envied his position.

Big was once the wide receiver who played for Columbia High. He had a very prominent future, but the streets had a hold on him; stealing his dreams. After many arrests, the press got involved, and his name being associated with fights and shootings, the school had to cut him from the team, to avoid scrutiny from the media. After that, Big dropped out of school and married the streets.

Scanning James's eyes and looking like he could read his soul, Big leaned in a little closer to him and said, "let me tell you about myself, James. I once played football for Columbia High and didn't have shit; always looking for a handout, loving this poor man's fame just like you," he said in a grim voice with a crooked smile.

For a second, Big seemed to struggle to pull hundreds of dollars from his Girbaud jeans, but succeeded, and intentionally started flicking small face hundreds off the top of his never-ending bills in the young star's face, taunting him while licking his lips, with a big grin.

"This is what I'm talking about, James; CASH!! The only difference between a football player on TV and me is that I can walk in the mall, freely, my nigga."

Big continued with his lecture, "This is MY city, Boy!!"

"You think they love you, don't you?"

"Makes you feel like the man, doesn't it?"

"Well let me be the first to tell you dog; they don't give a FUCK about you! Fuck up, hurt a leg or an arm, and your football dreams are done!"

"I do not hate on your new-found success, brother," he continued while shrugging his shoulder.

"I'm just trying to spare you before you get hurt, kid. I understand the importance of dreams, and I'm not trying to kill yours. I'm just telling you the truth, ya dig?!" Big said while grabbing James's wrist and shoving three hundred dollars in his palm.

James stared at the cash, thankful for the money he was given, but couldn't help but think that Big was stupid, and that's why he wasn't pro up till now. As bad as he wanted to say something, he kept his silence. Playing it smart and burying his voice, he just listened to Big mumbling on.

Big continued, saying, "What kind of life is this?!! Waiting for my little cousin to feed you?" Assuming they were broke and waiting for a handout.

"Hell, I know you ain't got no money, Lil nigga… with ya broke ass!" he said, knowing James's mother and her boyfriend were running a crack house not too far from his bar. His grim smile cut through his gold teeth as he continued, "Look bruh, I have a way out for you. I think you're a smart kid, and from experience, I know a quarterback is always a leader. Come and see me at the Bar, over on Boulevard when you ready to change your life; alright, Superstar?" Big said, winking his eye.

"Naw, I'm good," James replied, thinking of the consequences of that lifestyle. Besides, crack ruined his family's life, and he wasn't going to sell it to someone else's. He thanked Big for the money and join his friends at the table. He could not lie to himself, though. The proposition Big made did weigh heavy on his mind, but he tried to forget about it as he braced himself to take a seat with his friends. After joining them, he wondered why Big gave him the proposition and not his first cousin, Crazy Cory.

Then it crossed his mind! Cory liked to talk and could not keep any secrets. Crazy ass nigga, he thought, shaking his head. As he took his seat, he noticed the curious looks his friends had in their eyes.

"Man... what the hell, did he say, bru?"Cory asked while watching his cousin take a seat with his entourage in the corner of the Diner.

"Shiiiit, my nigga, he's talking about getting some money! He even gave me three hundred dollars!" said James, showing his money to his friends, triumphantly smiling and thumbing through his newfound riches.

"And what did YOU say?!" Killa Man asked with an over-excited look.

"I told him no!" said, James.

Crazy Cory and Killa Man had the same look on their faces. Their thoughts were transparent. James was a dumbass for turning down the opportunity of a lifetime.

"Man! This could have been our chance to come up!" Killa Man blurted out.

"Yeah, you are right," James replied and continued, "but football and the streets don't mix. Y'all saw what the hell happened to his dumbass. I don't know what y'all fools got on your minds, but I see myself in the NFL in the next four years."

Killa Man said, "Yeah, you right! But I'm sick of this broke shit, my nigga!"

With a graceful walk and a sparkling white smile, Grace held a tray of food over their table.

"You guys hungry?" she asked with a soft country accent as she laid the tray on the table. "My daddy said congratulations again on your winning the state, and he said to keep up the good work."

"Thanks," James said as he stood to tightly embrace her.

"Ya, thanks!" Killa Man said, trying to hug Grace after James, but before he could lift his arm in the air to embrace her, Grace held her palm in his face and said, "Naw, nigga!"

James knew no money would come until he made it to the NFL, despite the hundreds and thousands of dollars the school received through athletes annually from parents and students coming to see their team, win or lose. He realized, people had a way of distorting the truth; if you looked at it a little deeper, it's ALL a political lie. God forbid, if he tore a ligament or hurt his arm, his dreams would be crushed! He HAD to make it! A lot was going on in his mind for a seventeen-year-old. He didn't have a choice! He was forced to take care of his brother and sister, while his mom smoked dope! There was no other way out of his situation. Life was a game without a goal line. His mother's soul was torn between the streets and her kids, and she chose the closest thing to making her feel normal; the streets.

After he realized she was heartbroken and lost; trapped in a world where her sanity became lame to a life she once cherished, James had no choice, he had to make sure his siblings ate and were prepared for school every morning. His mother, once an attractive woman, with a coca-cola bottle shape, allowed crack to ruin her shape, along with her life. Her and her boyfriend Henry, continually watch their lives on the end of a crack pipe, go up in smoke. For James and his siblings that meant they were on their own. Once James realized there was no hope for his mother, he knew taking care of himself, and his younger siblings were his responsibility.

Before all this, Brenda's future was hopeful. She was viewed as a strong black female with a promising future as she focused on completing college. After graduating and having no choice but to move back home, she married her high school sweetheart, James Sr. Life got rough for her a few years later when tragedy struck, and their romance was short-lived, by his passing. James Sr. and Brenda started dating in high school when he was one of the most popular players on the football team. He loved the game of football, and the people in the city loved him. Brenda hated leaving him behind, but she felt her wings were too big for Columbia, South Carolina. People that stayed got stuck, and the ones that left, more than often came back down and out. She was determined to be one of the few to leave and never return. She graduated from high school and attended college in Atlanta, where she graduated with honors and a small cocaine habit. Coke gave her stamina to party on the weekends, and she used Adderall to focus during the week.

After graduating, she found it difficult to find work in her field due to her lack of experience. Jobless, broke, and lonely she moved back to the place she called home since birth, where she and the smooth-talking James Sr. didn't waste any time reconnecting. Once again, he swept her off her feet the moment she stepped foot in the city, and within months they were expecting their first child. A year later, they were husband and wife. They waited for some years to have their second child, and shortly after, a third one followed. Not long after the birth of their third child, James Sr. was involved in a head-on collision and left Brenda with three small children to raise all by herself, instantly, he was pronounced dead at the scene of the accident.

Brenda was devastated and took the news really hard. Full of grief, her college habit took the best of her as she started drinking and using cocaine heavily. Two years later, she managed to find the "devil" himself, in the form of a tall, skinny and persuasive crack head, named Henry. Henry started coming by her house often to get high and play cards. He was always well dressed, with the gift of gab. Eloquent words that definitely got Brenda's attention. Henry fell in love with Brenda the first time he laid eyes on her. She was highly favored amongst everyone, but Henry admired her intelligence along with her smooth caramel skin, short and sexy posture, and long black silky hair. Brenda had an attitude, only a mother would love, but Henry didn't care for her feisty mouth. He was one of the few who could handle her and knew exactly how to shut her up.

Dope was a severe epidemic in the '90s, and if your parents were not on it, more than likely they sold it or knew someone who did. James and his siblings knew about it all too well. Henry was one of the contributors, trying to sell crack here and there, to keep up with his habits. Because of him, junkies would hang around the house day in and day out, and he did not care how this affected Brenda's kids. Even Brenda no longer made them a priority. Feeding them was the last thing on her mind, so school became their rest haven — a place where they could get a hot meal and play in peace.

Most school nights, they were able to endure the chaotic environment their mother created at home, but on weekends, no one could get much sleep when their home became the gathering place for anyone craving a fix. The aroma of crack and the stench of alcohol constantly filled the air along with loud chatter of those hanging around to enjoy Henry's product. When he had really good dope, their front door revolved all night!! Sometimes for days from junkies craving another fix. Some faces were familiar to James, but most were strangers, so he did his best to protect his siblings from the chaos surrounding them.

Brenda's habit had gotten worse over the years. The kids would cry in their older brother's arms whenever they realized that their favorite toys had suddenly disappeared. These were the times he wished they could wake up in another area code. The refrigerator was rarely full. Brenda received food stamps but sold the majority to local dope boys to support her life-changing habit. The shit that was going on with Brenda and Henry would make any child grow up fast, regardless of who they were. James was no exception to the rules. The responsibility of his brother and sister solely rested in his hands, and that's why the NFL became a priority to the young superstar. His ultimate goal was to get his mother some help and move his siblings from this "hell" they called life.

CHAPTER 2
The Hunt

A Coach Roper stepped from the all-black F150, he thought of how much he hated going to see the redneck. As a white coach of an all-black football team, he had grown to love and respect, his players. Roper hated the white supremacist ways of old Mayor Ford. He knew he would hear him sing the same old song about what the Mayor called a loyal relationship with the 28-year-old coach's father, John Roper, who served on the local police force when he was alive. Back then, Mayor Ford was the Chief of police, and John Roper, the Deputy, was his right-hand man. There were many nights those two just sat on Roper's dad's porch drinking scotch, chasing it with beer, mixed with endless discussions about the Blacks and Mexicans; blaming them for all the problems of the world.

Roper's father terrorized the hood for years. No one was safe. He was well known for taking what wasn't his and beating anyone who opposed him. Often, he even went as far as killing whenever he had an opportunity or command to do so. He was really good at following the Chief's instructions, and whatever Chief Ford told him to do, he did without complaining. Sometimes, Roper's mother and father would get into heated arguments about his father's occupation. It wasn't because he was a cop, but mainly because of his side-hustle. A hustle that would ultimately lead to his demise. Roper's father and his "gang" were known for ripping off Mexicans and African Americans for years. They did it with or without the Chief's permission. His loyalty to the Chief was uncertain at times. He skimmed money off the top to support his cocaine and poker habit, which became very expensive over time. He forced his family to live below their means, which caused him to put in overtime doing crime. He and a few other fellow officers, a force of seven, would torture low-income neighborhoods to fill their stomachs with profits.

The Chief, along with his gang, The Lone Rangers, ran the criminal underworld. They helped open a gate; they later found would be impossible to close or control. Their greed took them from stick-ups to introducing crack cocaine to the streets of Columbia. The entire staff was corrupt, and Ford was king of the chessboard. Whatever he told his guys to do they did, no questions asked. They saw what happened to people that double-crossed the Chief or couldn't obey simple instructions.

Everyone in the community knew that it was a setup when Roper's Father was found shot and burned under a rarely used bridge. They came up with their own version of the truth, to satisfy their curiosities. The police had to find someone to blame for this horrific crime, so they decided to apprehend three black teens and charge them with murder, giving them life on death row. The young Roper couldn't eat or sleep for months. He was only 15. His father's death was devastating, and it haunted him for the longest time.

After the passing of Roper's father, the Mayor and his mother became close, and he started coming around more often than usual. He eventually took the young Roper under his wing, showing him the ropes in hopes he could have him under his feet just like his dad. But, young Roper had plans of his own and became rebellious. He eventually went off to college in Atlanta to study criminal law. Roper was only able to remain in school for two short years. After his mother's diagnosis of cancer, he had no choice but to return home to take care of her. It did not take long before his mother passed away from cancer and a lonely heart.

Roper never expected his family ties to lead him into the darkest places in society. His dreams were to finish college, but after the death of both of his parents; Chief Ford became the closest thing to family to him. The Chief knew Roper. Just like his father, greed would become his motivation. Their desire was a family curse, and the Chief knew how to keep him fully satisfied. With nothing else to look forward to, Roper quickly followed in his dad's footsteps and became the Mayor's crony.

It was a wintery morning, in a secluded room on Capitol Hill, when Ford and his staff members gathered to discuss the epic cocaine issue that plagued their city. The rate of crime was high, and dirty money lined the pockets of drug dealers across the country. A few of the politicians made jokes about getting a nigger to sell their drugs. Ford laughed out loud but secretly thought it was a great idea. He had planned to get Roper in the police department to become his eyes and ears;

someone he could trust and keep a close tab on. But Ford's plan took a detour when Roper decided to become a coach, working with underprivileged kids of the ghetto. The Mayor was furious about Roper's decision, but Roper's mind was made up, and there was nothing he could do to change it. The Mayor thought that maybe this was not such a bad idea, after all, because he still had Roper where he wanted him in the black community.

Roper was going through changes of his own and started experiencing real financial hardship, which set the chessboard perfectly in Ford's favor. Ford managed to work around Roper, not becoming Columbia's finest and decided to hire one of his pals from his old department, offering him the position of Chief. Although he now had the Chief in his pocket and half of the city hall, Roper was still the only piece missing. The key to the streets.

Roper stepped out of the elevator, fixing his suit and tie, he mentally prepared himself before entering the grandmaster's office. Before Roper could open the office door, the wrinkled-face man, whose breath reeked of scotch and cigars, met him there. His belly was similar to a man who watched TV and drunk beer all day. Roper squeezed passed him as he entered the room and proceeded to take a seat in his huge, nicely kept office. Following Roper, the Mayor grabbed a cigar from his breast pocket and took a seat on the corner of his desk. He lit it up, then took a long puff. He pulled the Cuban cigar from his mouth and stared at it in admiration.

"You know you're one damn good coach, Roper," Ford said sarcastically as he blew thick clouds of smoke in the atmosphere, "But if you can't control that nigga Curtis, I will!"

"Excuse me," Roper said as he fanned the cigar smoke from his face.

"Curtis owes me over a hundred thousand dollars, not to mention, he's playing cowboys and Indians, totally demolishing my deal with the doctor. This is making all of us look bad, Roper," the very frustrated Mayor said in a tone that echoed through his office.

Roper sighed, then mumbled, "you are overcharging the poor fellow by twenty grand."

Realizing Roper's mumble, Ford became hostile. It was clear that he was becoming agitated. Mayor Ford's face turned beet red with anger while attempting to put his cigar out in the ashtray on his desk. The Mayor was confused as to why Roper would give these blacks so much respect when he was the one that practically raised him. He was nothing in the Mayor's eyes, just like his father. He was convinced that Roper, just like everyone else on his payroll, would never gain a level of success without him. He made them all rich, including that black ass Curtis.

"Don't be a jackass, Roper!" the Mayor continued, still smothering the cigar in the ashtray.

"Speaking from a logical perspective, how long do you think we can get away with this Ford? For goodness sake, you owe people from Congress to the damn street kids, and I'm the one taking the fucking slack," Roper said, throwing the street kids' bit in for good measure.

Understanding Roper's frustration, Ford humbled himself while retrieving two shot glasses from the cupboard and said, "Son, you don't get it, do you? You've been coaching these little, colored boys for years. You know you can't control Curtis no more than when you were his damn coach."

Roper had seen this look in Ford's eyes before. Masked by a pathetic act of kindness, as he watched the old, greasy, slime bucket pour two shots of scotch, he could see the hatred in his eyes. His life was on the line every time he faced Curtis. He knew Ford was only driven by greed and would never look at the big picture. Roper decided to drop the subject, letting Ford continue to paint his father's name in a good light as if he was a top cop. Roper had heard these stories over a million times and was sick of the "good cop" routine Ford would throw around about his father. He saw them both as political killers that turned communities into chaos, and he was forced in the middle of it all.

Nevertheless, Ford was right; they created a Frankenstein: a real monster. Curtis was known to leave stiffs throughout the entire city. Some were innocent people, casualties of war. It wouldn't be too long before the "alphabet boys" would start asking questions. Roper thought, maybe Curtis was just as ruthless as Mayor Ford and his father, entertaining thoughts of murdering his understudy.

Ford poured them both another shot, then said, "Face it, son, the boy has to die! There are plenty of poor negros lined up around the city ready to take his place."

Staring at the syrupy liquor, Roper's thoughts took him to when he coached Curtis. He was an extraordinary kid: one with a great deal of talent. If it wasn't for his short fuse, he might have had opportunities to do something productive with his life. Roper chugged his shot thinking he would never allow someone like Curtis to ruin his life. As far as he was concerned, he gave Curtis opportunities to do the right thing, and he fucked up each time. Roper could finally see Ford's point of view concerning Curtis and surprisingly found himself agreeing with the Mayor on his fate.

The Mayor was involved in everything. His hand extended everywhere in the city from the KKK to dirty judges, politicians, and cops. He blackmailed them all! He ran Columbia, South Carolina, with an iron fist and silver bullets. And he wanted Curtis dead; his body to disappear, and never to be seen again. Some families got a chance to view their loved one's body out of respect. Ford only made a few exceptions. His "kills" were untraceable, and when families did have a chance to see the body, it had to appear as if their death was accidental and no foul play. Most of his constituents feared him. They stood on eggshells at the sight of him, adhering to his every command. Power was what made Ford's blood boil as fresh lava dipped straight from hell. The more influence he gained, the more destructive he became destroying the lives of those who crossed him.

Roper was well aware of Ford's capabilities and preferred not to have any parts in his dark side. There were silent rumors around the police department. Rumors that Ford had a hand in his father's death, but the majority denied those rumors. Most believed Ford was a good man and would never do such a thing to one of his own. But Roper knew better; Ford was capable of just about anything. Besides, this wouldn't be the first time Ford asked him to do his dirty work and kill someone. Roper's hands weren't clean, but he hated the thought of killing a kid he mentored for years. It made him feel as if he was signing his name in blood. Was he once again selling his soul to the devil and digging a hole for himself as deep as the bottomless pit? Once upon a time, his desire was to help the inner-city kids, not kill them.

However, Roper realized the grip the mayor had on his life and responded reluctantly, "I'm in," as he stood up and prepared to leave.

Before Roper could get out of the office, Ford called out, "O yeah! Good game you guys played, son!" Raising his hand in the air waving Roper off.

Roper's goal was to get a hold of Curtis before any other casualties took place. He wasted no time and called him from his custom-made car phone.

Several seconds went by before Curtis answered.

"Hey, Big! What's happening, bro?" Roper said, using Curtis's street name. Finding it ridiculous why grown people would ever call him "Big."

Big answered, "What's up, coach?" simultaneously pointing to the exit as two beautiful women departed his bed.

Roper took a deep sigh, thinking this may be the last conversation he would ever have with Curtis. He said, "You need to meet me at the park; the same spot, in an hour."

"Alright!" Big said. Then he hung up the phone.

Roper sat on a bench in a deserted park. Although it was around the first of the year, the temperature was warm, and the beauty of Mother Nature soothed his mind from the chaos that was surrounding him. His thoughts wandered off in time when he coached the summer league football team in this very park before they thought it would be more suitable as a soccer field and walking trail. After a few moments of waiting around, Roper stretched his arm to check the time on his Rolex. Seconds later, he noticed Big walking down the sidewalk in a tailored suit with a gangsta's bop in his stride. Big's goons were nowhere in sight, but Roper knew they weren't far. Not giving Big any time to get comfortable, he jumped straight to business.

"We have a serious problem, Curtis," Roper said reading Big's eyes and body language, figuring he could fly off the deep end at any moment.

Big knew they were overcharging him by twenty grand, leaving him the crumbs compared to what they were making. But, twenty grand was a small price, considering the fact that everyone got envelopes stuffed with hundreds to keep his black ass out of jail.

The task was clear! Get Big to stop filling the streets with stiffs at least until he found someone to replace him. He thought of making the replacement do his dirty work to show loyalty. He smiled at the devious thought crossing his mind. It was a flawless operation. They evaporated corpses with ease, and if only Big played along, they all would have been rich. Big refusing to cooperate, held them from millions. The few bodies they received were riddled with bullets. The doctor didn't have a problem with one or two bullet holes, but the corpses Big was calling in, were severely damaged. Major organs were shredded, leaving them useless. Big was reckless, and his goons were even worse. They had careless kills with no morals. Sometimes the innocent were caught in the crossfire. Drive-bys' and freelance shootings painted bloody stains on the streets of Columbia.

Big's eyes were bloodshot red as he stared Roper down with a cold glare, wondering what excuse he would have for overcharging him this time. It was clear that Roper and his constituents were greedy, and he was sick of getting crumbs. Besides, these were HIS streets! Without him, Roper and his fucking constituents wouldn't be rich anyway.

With pure arrogance, Big asked, "What is it this time, Roper?" Expecting bullshit to pour from Roper's mouth like vomit.

Noticing his frustration, Roper calmed his tone to change the mood. The last thing he wanted was for Big's goons to come running down the hill. He was a businessman and only killed when necessary. He didn't even own a gun but wished he had in his current situation. For a moment, he felt he was prey. Fearing the worst, while noticing the animosity in Big's eyes

(Not to mention, the two-armed men standing in front of a car on the hill he could now see). Finally, Roper mustered up the balls to speak his mind.

"Curtis, you have to chill, man! You're going to have the FBI and every other "alphabet" snooping around here, looking for answers, man!" said Roper pleading his case.

Still coldly peering into Roper's pupils, Big smiled. He realized Roper knew nothing about what went down in his neck of the woods. All Roper could see was an easy check for him to cash in on. He was his mule, a puppet; a means to his financial gain.

Big proceeded, calmly, asking Roper if his visit was really about the Feds or when he saw dead black bodies, did he only think 'cash'?

Changing the subject, Roper's response was, "Talent is what I see in a lot of you black guys." He went on to patronize Big by saying he once had talent until he became a common thug who cared about nothing but his self-interest. Being a coach was just a part of Roper's M.O. But fucking with people's heads was just something he was great at. Big's demeanor slowly changed. The more Roper spoke, the more confident he became in surviving the meeting.

"Look, Curtis, there's no better way to say it. You're out of control. You have dead bodies showing up in the middle of the streets for God's sake." Feeling his anxiety diminish; Roper continued to fuss.

"We've been doing business for a long time. I've been coaching you since you were in the ninth grade. Trust me, and I wouldn't tell you anything that would affect you negatively, son!" Leaning closer to gain Big's undivided attention, Roper continued, "When the FBI and CIA and all the other three-letter agencies start snooping around your ass, you will be the one to pay the piper."

Before he knew it, he had his finger shoved in Big's shoulder as he spoke boldly, "and guess what? I'll be in my beautiful suite, drinking a nice cold beer, watching your crazy ass on the five o'clock news, man! Besides, who do you think let your murder spree continue for all these years," asked Roper, winking one eye. He would never let the situation get that far as the Feds, but he thought mentioning the FBI would buy him some time from Big's murder spree.

Moving Roper's finger from his shoulder, Big snapped, telling him not to fucking touch him.

Frankly, he was sick of Roper's shit. Who the hell did he think HE was!? Telling him how to control his hood? Big's blood boiled!!! He wanted to snap this man's finger in half but held his composure. Despite the fact, he was being overcharged and now disrespected; it had to be business first. Why risk thousands of dollars over twenty grand and a poke in the shoulder? Big kept his feelings in check and held vengeance in his heart. He saved money over time and had his plans to get away from what he called a fake ass coach and his mysterious friends. They were scavengers picking pennies from the cracks of concrete where he once stayed.

Big was no pillar of the community, but the thought of his former coach making huge profits by killing innocent kids he once coached, made his skin crawl. The coach was the one always "preaching" integrity, hard work, and sacrifice, but he knew that was just bullshit! He had to admit that he was a damn good coach but a fucked-up human being. This man was as shady as they came. Although he wasn't the person pulling the trigger, blood flowed through Roper's fingers just as it did his.

After minutes of debating, neither one of them could see eye to eye. They exchanged foul language at a respectable tone, keeping their cool. They both wanted to cut ties, drawing the line, not knowing how far the red brick road would take them. Destruction and death were all they had in store for each other – Once the student and a coach were now competition, that could turn deadly.

CHAPTER 3
A Hard Life

James and his mother Brenda sat quietly on the old worn-out sofa, watching cartoons while his siblings played on the fairly clean carpet. The house was unusually quiet. Usually, there would be crack friends knocking on the door as they do day in and day out.

Henry didn't mind it being slow. It gave him a chance to prepare his day. He was in the bedroom, busy cutting pebbles from the slab of dope with an old dirty razor he found in the dresser drawer. He sacked the pieces in small baggies. He thought he had a few crumbs of crack left in his pocket from last night's smoke fest and hoped to smoke the crumbs to get his day started.

A breaking news bulletin flashed across the bottom screen of the old floor model TV, interrupting the cartoons. Brenda quickly hushed the chattering kids to hear the news. The police who allegedly caught a seventeen-year-old armed black male breaking in his patrol car gunned him down. The officer said he saw the young man while he and his partner were purchasing a cup of coffee. Dropping his cup, he raced out of the store as fast as he could, only to see the teen had gotten a good running start. He yelled, "Stop! "Stop!" but the teen refused. Once the suspect halted and turned around, he opened fire in fear the teen had stolen one of his firearms from the patrol car. He continued saying that it was a good thing he acted in such a timely fashion because the suspect had indeed stolen his firearm. He had no choice but to shoot him five times. He intended to "injure" not to "kill," the officer told the news, without an ounce of remorse.

James shook his head while his mother stared at the old floor model TV in disbelief. The police patrolled their communities without any respect as if they couldn't see any good in black faces. They constantly scanned the streets for their next victim, to beat or to take to jail on trumped-up charges. People were getting sick of it, but what could they do?

"This shit is a damn shame! Another parent has to bury their child," said Brenda while grabbing the lighter and cigarettes from the coffee table. She was terrified at the thought of that being her child on the news. Kids dying in the street seemed to happen too often in Columbia. A lot had changed from when she was just a little girl.

After searching through his jeans, he had on the night before, and Henry began to get angry. He lashed out in rage, slamming the bedroom door. His footsteps echoed from the hollow floor, disturbing the long-awaited peace of mind James and his mother were clearly enjoying.

"Brenda! Brenda! Where's my shit from last night?" Henry screamed as he aggressively approached Brenda.

She quickly pushed herself off the worn screeching couch and shouted, "How the hell... am I supposed to know, Henry?" She boldly stared in his eyes, thinking about the worst outcome.

Sometimes Henry got so high he forgot he misplaced, lost, or smoked his dope. When he came to his senses the next day, he would often terrorize Brenda when he couldn't find his shit. This happened often, and Brenda was always the prime suspect. There was the look of a mad man in Henry's eyes. His body fiend for an afternoon buzz. He had bagged what he wanted to sell and wanted to avoid smoking his profit. He was certain he had a few crumbs of crack left and was now blaming Brenda; the only person blocking his path to a morning high. The more they fussed, the tenser the argument got.

Henry lunged on top of Brenda and said, "You, dumb bitch! It was in my pockets last night… I know where I keep my shit!"

Before Brenda could respond, his fist was in the air, and his palm gripped her voice box. Henry was choking the life out of her on the couch. She gasped for air, trying to yell for him to stop, but the grip around her neck made it difficult for her to breath. Brenda did all she could to shove Henry off her but failed at her efforts. His weight overpowered the petite woman, whose fights were full of fire. She was frustrated with Henry. She was determined to put up a fight; tired of this man's uncontrollable rage and physical abuse. His fist crashed down on her face, bursting a blood vessel in one eye.

Fed up with the commotion, James football tackled Henry, knocking him off his mother. The other kids stood at a distance, watching the "entertainment." This wasn't the first time they saw their mother being abused by Henry. But, this was the first time their brother fought back, and they were all amazed at his strength. Although they remained quiet, the glare of excitement shined in their eyes as they watched James force Henry into the black china cabinet that stood counter corner to the wall. The few dishes on the shelves of the cabinet fell to the floor, creating a loud crash.

"Stop!" Brenda yelled at the sight of the chaos, asking both men to please calm down.

Ignoring her cries, James continued to shove Henry, forcing the kids to shift to the opposite side of the living room.

"James, please stop!" cried Brenda, pleading for him to lay off her abuser.

Fueled with retaliation, James snapped as he whaled punches to Henry's face, refusing to let him recover. The abuse had been going on for years, and enough was enough. Today he would show Henry, this was his home his father left for his family, and Henry would respect his mother for as long as he lived there.

Overpowered and out of breath, Henry gave up, laying on his back and spreading his arms on the floor as a sign of surrender. After seeing the gesture, James immediately jumped to his feet to prepare for round two.

Knowing the battle was lost; Henry thought it would be in his best interest to just explain himself. After dusting off the debris from the carpet, he gave the best explanation he could think of.

"James, your momma stole my dope she's a fuckin crackhead!" he said while pointing his finger in Brenda's direction, with the right side of his upper lip pointing towards his nose.

He sucked his teeth and said, "You know I would never do anything to hurt your momma, or the kids!" glancing at the babies chuckling while wiping the blood from his nose.

"It was all bullshit," James thought. Out of all the games he had won in pee-wee to the state championship trophies that lined the top of his dresser, standing up to Henry made him feel the most accomplished. His mom used to be so beautiful and loving before she met this crackhead. Now drugs and neglect were all she had to give. He hated what his mother had become, and his heart brewed with equal hatred towards the very man he thought destroyed their lives with the "devil's" addiction.

Noticing his pleads to James weren't working, Henry focused his attention on Brenda. Feeling embarrassed because he'd just got his ass whooped by his stepson, he said, "Bitch! That's your fucking problem you got no control over these damn kids."

They were all staring at him as he tried to control the blood flowing from his nose with his t-shirt. It gave Brenda great relief to see James handle himself as a man. This was long overdue. She was tired of getting pounded on, even though most of the time she really did smoke all of Henry's dope. After all, he lived in her house, and after the bills he paid, dope was just tax. She stood proudly, but with a visible sign of guilt on her face, daring Henry to touch her again. Her son was finally grown enough to fight her battles.

A heavy knock on the metal barred door sliced through the tension in the room, bringing the loud fussing and fighting to a silence.

"This ain't over, little nigga," Henry mumbled, bumping James's shoulder as he mugged Brenda.

"Who is it?" said Henry loud but exhausted after fighting with the 180-pound teenager.

"It's Clyde! Open up, man!" the short skinny junky yelled from outside.

Clyde and Henry had been friends for a long time. They were known for robbing stations and running a couple of cons together back in the day. Everyone from the neighborhood knew the fast-talking hustler for befriending people just to steal from them, earning him the nickname "Klepto Clyde." Dusting the dirt off his dingy white tee, Henry shook his head. He stared hard at Brenda, wanting her to feel awful for the ass whooping he endured. Brenda simply rolled her eyes and looked towards the door, suggesting he should answer it. She could sense his reluctance as he slowly walked outside and slammed the door behind him.

Blowing off Henry's remarks, James hugged his mom. As Brenda embraced her son, she smiled with pride, stepping back while holding his arms and cracking a warm-hearted smile. She could feel her eyes swelling from the abuse she just endured, but she wanted him to know how much she admired his courage. She couldn't fight and felt awful for dragging her family in such a chaotic situation. She knew that ninety percent of their fights were because she stole crumbs from Henry's stash. She didn't mind taking brutal abuse. Most of the time, she was high and could barely feel the abrasions anyway.

For a moment, James thought he captured his mother's full attention. In his mind, he prepared a motivational speech for her, but the moment only lasted a second. Noticing her focus leaning more towards what was going on outside, you could see the disappointment and disgust on his facial expression. Pushing her hands off his arm, he mumbled, "fuck it!", as he walked into a room, he shared with his siblings. James thought of the better days before his mother met Henry. She was a great mom, who was deeply concerned about her children's education and future. Crack was a very dangerous weapon against the black community. It split families and destroyed their future; it didn't care about your race, age, or gender. It only demanded your greed, from the sellers and smokers alike.

Henry stormed into the house and grabbed Brenda by the arm; escorting her to their room and closing the door behind them. Not knowing Henry's intentions and refusing to let him get the "drop" on her, Brenda quickly prepared herself for round two. Checking out her fighting stance, Henry glared at her and chuckled.

After getting her to calm down, he asked if her cousin still had possession of the gun he'd tried to sell to him a few weeks back. Only hearing the word "gun," she asked if he was stupid? Mimicking his silly chuckle, she ridiculed him and asked what he was going to do with a gun? Kill himself? Quickly switching the conversation, she asked Henry if Clyde had anything to smoke. Not wanting to ask him for any, so fresh off an ass whooping. Besides, she figured she'd smoked his last anyway.

Henry glared at Brenda in disbelief, thinking there was no hope for her; he yelled in frustration, "Naw! You fuckin' junkie!"

Taking offense to Henry's insult, Brenda crossed her arms, rolled her eyes, and sucked her teeth as she yelled back, "I ain't no fuckin' junkie!"

"I am so ready to end this conversation," she mumbled under her breath while fixing the thin spaghetti strap leaning from her shoulder.

"Damn you, Brenda! I don't have time to be fuckin' with your ass Now, do your cuz have the damn pistol, or what?" Henry said in a lower voice; in an attempt to calm his tone.

Skeptical, Brenda said, "I don't know, but I will find out! What you need a gun for, Henry?"

Not wanting to say too much, Henry sighed. While looking into Brenda's red-eye that had already started developing a black ring around it, he continued, "Clyde got a plan to get some real money baby, so I'm going to need that gun... ASAP! Ok?!" He tried being sincere, hoping he would get the right answer this time around, and Brenda shook her head, in agreement with Henry's request.

The next morning, to avoid getting into a lengthy and probably useless dialog over the phone, Roper drove to the Mayor's mansion to give him some unwanted news. Telling the old man that Big wasn't cooperating, was a death warrant, and he was glad he was on the opposite end of the gun. Getting his words in order before hell rained in his ears, Roper reluctantly approached the door. To his surprise, Ford greeted him with open arms. 'He must be in one of his rare good moods,' he thought.

"There he goes, just the man I was waiting for." The Mayor smiled, showing his pearly white dentures. He threw his arm around Roper's shoulder, and escorted him into the house.

A sweet aroma of fresh garlic and pasta was coming from the kitchen. His home was beautiful. No one in this entire town lived as extravagant as Mayor Ford. This guy lived like the "Godfather" with maids, chauffeurs, and goons. The whole nine yards!

"Follow me into the den son and tell me how yesterday went. After a morning like this, I could use some good news," the Mayor said, skeptical of the information he was about to receive.

"Well!" Roper sighed, folding his arms, "I got news alright, but it's not good news. I spoke with Curtis, and he didn't take the news lightly, and frankly, Ford, he's pissed for being overcharged! If you ask me, I think he has something else he's working on," Roper said as he proceeded to walk towards the den.

"Goddammit Roper! You incompetent son of a bitch. I told you to get your little nigger puppet in order!! You are fucking weaker than a paraplegic's legs, Son!" Shouted Ford, making a gesture for Roper to take a seat once they reached the den.

"If I were in your shoe, son, he would've been hanging on God's green earth a long time ago!" Ford said, waiting for Roper to take a seat before he continued.

The racial rhetoric and disrespect made Roper not wanting to stick around long enough to sit down. But "NO!" wasn't the answer Ford was looking for. When Ford gave a second nod towards the oversized armchair, motioning for Roper to make himself comfortable, he took a seat in an attempt not to prolong his stay with a useless argument over his comfort. Curtis was drunk in his way, just like the old man, and he saw neither one of them sobering up. Both were crazed with greed and murder, and he was stuck in the middle, relaying messages back and forth.

Mayor Ford didn't bother sitting down. He walked slowly to the kitchen to retrieve his bulky cell phone from his black overcoat draping from a chair. Thinking of a phrase his father once told him, "The only way your standards and your goals get met is when you make them meet." Although Ford and his father's relationship was less than perfect, a lot of his dad's teachings haunted his ways and left a blueprint for his life. He grabbed his reading glasses from the countertop and squinted his eyes to retrieve a number from his cell phone. Ford thought of how weak Roper was as he held his mobile device.

'If the Feds ever got involved,' Roper would 'sing like a canary.' It was time for him to bust his cherry and kill that nigger himself," he thought. He figured it would give Roper a little incentive to keep his mouth shut if their time ever expired. Ford slipped his cell phone back in the overcoat. Thinking it was time to do away with this nigger, they called Big, once and for all.

Turning around, just in time to catch eyes with his middle age Hispanic maid, he said, "Maria! Maria! You are always on time, sweetheart," directing her to the cupboard to fix a couple of shots of bourbon for himself and Roper.

Ford met Roper in the den, followed by his maid carrying shots of whiskey. After giving them their shots of bourbon, Roper waited for the maid to close the door behind her. He didn't waste any time telling Ford the loopholes in his plans. He explained he didn't have anyone to replace Curtis just yet, and it would be damn near impossible to find someone on such short notice. Without even so much as a blink, Ford took a sip from his shot glass before cutting into Roper's doubt with a little sarcasm and asked if he was still using cocaine. He even threw gas on the fire and called him "Coach" with a devious smirk. Judging by the lost look on Roper's face, along with a soft sniff, Ford had his answer. He figured Roper was still using, flushing a small percentage of their profit up his nose. Lifting his finger, trying to explain himself, Roper was quickly interrupted with fake compassion. Ford firmly gripped Roper's shoulder, piercing his soul with eye contact, telling him he 'understood how stressful his job could be' and he 'did what he had to do' to take the edge off.

"Right?" Ford said, looking for confirmation, toasting Roper's glass.

Not understanding where Ford's conversation was headed, Roper gave an insincere smile and chugged his shot. With false sincerity in his voice, Ford told Roper how great of an asset he was, not only to him but also to the kids he coached. Then he reminded him of how he has always been there for him, like family. Noticing Roper beginning to see through his bullshit, Ford cut straight to the point, unveiling the true nature of their conversation.

"Even a dumbass can come up with a bright idea every once in a while, Son! So, I'm sure you finding a replacement won't be an issue, right Roper?" Taking a deep sigh, Ford continued, "The bottom line is, Son, Curtis is a liability, and if you don't deal with him soon, both our asses will be in a vice."

Roper had a small issue with killing Curtis. He didn't want to go to prison behind his trigger-happy ass, and it wasn't like Curtis was Roper's first kill. Thinking one step ahead, he kept Ford in the dark about a lot of things knowing his blackmail methods could be ruthless and unforgiving. He owed Curtis for saving his life once, and besides, it bothered him to kill the kid he had mentored on and off the football field.

"What exactly do you mean by you," Roper said, pointing his thumb towards his chest, confused. "I thought you had people to deal with these type of situations!"

Sitting down in the large armchair across from Roper, Ford said with a dry confession, "Yes, I do, but I think it's time you start skinning your own fish, Son."

"No, No, No! Fuck that shit!" Roper said. "I've coached that boy since high school; now you want me to kill him?" He was definitely feeling sick at the thought of murdering his own pupil.

As Roper stood from his comfortable seat, Ford said, "Sit down, Son," expecting Roper's reaction. Ford's demeanor was calm, but a sense of urgency smothered the room as he convinced Roper that his decision was best for everyone.

"You know I always thought you would be a better cop than a drug dealer or coach. It turns out, the only thing you're good at is reporting bad news," Ford said as he continued with his insults.

Ford mumbled, just loud enough to where Roper could hear him, "My career and my life are in the hands of your nigga from across the tracks."

Shaking his head and finger from side to side, Ford raised his raspy country voice, "This shit is your problem. You let Curtis get carried away!" he said, pointing his wrinkled finger at Roper. "We have an iron-clad deal worked out with Dr. Williams. Why isn't he using him? That's what he's there for!!! Goddam cleanups!" Calming down to give himself time to think, the Mayor poured another shot of whiskey while staring at Roper to make sure he had his attention..

"You know, it's one thing I can't understand Roper? You work with these inner-city kids for all these years. Last I remember you're a coach and a coach knows how to adjust his team in a tight situation Right?"

Roper regretted getting himself involved or even entertaining this conversation. However, he also knew rejecting Ford could be his demise as a coach and potentially ruin his life as a drug dealer. He witnessed the downfall of people's lives. His back was against the wall, and his nuts were the ones in the vice grip. Watching as Roper nodded his head in arrogance, the Mayor boldly continued, "See, the problem here is, we don't see conflict the same way. You try to run from your problems, and I attack them," Ford said, slamming his fist in his palm. "Besides," said the Mayor, as he walked around Roper, patting him on the shoulder with a grimy voice of vision, "Every last one of them negroes would love to spread their wings in my enterprise. Now go, work on getting me another one; because this negro's pathetic life is coming to an end. Now if you will excuse me."

The Mayor motioned for Roper to get out of his seat and shoved him towards the door. "I have work to do, and the People don't like excuses."

As Roper walked out the door, he thought they were no better than the "have nots" of the ghetto. Instead of the Mayor using his power to enforce change into the communities, he used drugs to control the streets. He also thought of his moral compass and how it didn't point north. The coach frowned and rubbed his forehead as if he had a migraine and thought of the death he was selling to this young man he was supposed to mentor. The money was great, but he hated the Mayor, who had his hook buried under his skin. With a smirk, he debunked his thoughts - who was he fooling; it wasn't the hooks of the Mayor that kept him going; it was the money, women, and cocaine that had him in the frying pan with a scorched soul. The moment Roper reached his truck, he dumped half a gram in the dimple of his closed fist, then treated his nose to a little "candy." As much as he hated Curtis, the thought of his blood on his hands made his stomach swirl.

The strong aroma of crack [cocaine]filled the air in the small, dingy kitchen. Wide-eyed and fidgety, Clyde took a swallow of his cheap liquor as he attempted to bring down a high that made his bottom lip shift constantly while Henry shoveled the deck of cards looking to break a 'crack fiend's' silence.

"Hay! How much money you got," asked Henry while dealing the cards. Clyde was in no position to gamble but patted his pockets even though he knew there wasn't a dollar there.

Clyde managed to muster, "Nothing, I... I... I... I'm a broke man," chewing on his top lip as he scooped the cards in his hands. Even though he had no money, Clyde was known for always running a scheme to satisfy his habits and pockets. Tonight was no different, except they weren't knocking off a liquor store or stealing a purse. The consequences could be deadly, for both of them.

"Speaking of broke," Henry said while pulling a 38 snub nose from his jacket pocket hanging from the back of the chair, he continued, "...what's the plan again?" slamming the pistol on the wooden table, creating a loud thump.

They played blackjack as Clyde explained his crazy game plan. The mention of Big's name made Henry's skin crawl. He quickly interrupted Clyde's plans for a one-way ticket to an early grave. Henry sarcastically repeated Clyde's words to him so he could hear how stupid his plans were. Usually, Clyde would come up with some crazy airtight cons, but this was by far the dumbest one yet. Lifting his palm in the air while holding a card between his fingers, Clyde insisted Henry listened to him. He explained he had a person on the inside that he could trust, and they've been working on their plan for a few months. The only thing he and Henry had to do was snatch Big up, drop him off in the country, and they would do the rest. Before Clyde could even finish with the kidnapping part, Henry was already out his seat shaking his head, "no."

He thought Clyde had lost his mind! There was no way they could pull this off. Big had too much muscle, and they only had one gun, with no car. Henry had almost made his final decision that is until Clyde mentioned his cut.

"We could get over fifty grand a piece if everything goes right," Clyde said, rubbing his hands together in sheer greed.

"Fifty Grand?!" Henry asked, entertaining the thought while staring at the gun in front of him.

"Fifty Grand!" Clyde repeated, smiling while noticing his partner in crime was considering coming aboard.

Still not fully convinced, Henry asked, "Where in the hell would we take him with no car?! And who the fuck is this inside nigga you talking about?"

Not wanting to reveal his source, Clyde carefully responded, "Settle down, man! I got this under control! The hideout is damn not too far, in the other side of the state, somewhere deep in the country. No one would look for him where we're going. Besides, everything is set! You in or out, Man?" said Clyde, grabbing the burner off the table.

"Clyde!" Henry demanded, snatching the gun from him, "Are you sure you can trust these cats?"

Sick of Henry's paranoia, instead of a verbal response, Clyde gave him a reassuring stare. "All we have to do is drop him off and they will take care of the rest. We collect our Fifty Grand on the drop and just like that; easy money! So, what you say?! You in or what, Henry?"

The risk was big, but the reward was greater, Henry thought, as he ground his teeth. Trying to keep his high under control, he repeated to Clyde their plan and emphasize, "All we have to do is drop him off and get the money!"

Clyde shook his head and said, "ya, ya, ya, but there is just one problem."

"Got-damn, Clyde!" Henry said. "What?!"

"We only have two days and Monday is our best time to make it happen," Clyde said, lighting up his last cigarette.

Henry chuckled and said, "Clyde, this some crazy shit, man!" Henry knew, once Big made it to the country, he would never come back. The word was that they fed people to hogs out there as a way of disposing all evidence and traces.

CHAPTER 4
The Mule

*M*ndays were usually slow at the bar, especially because it was closing time. From the outside, you wouldn't think much of the building with its old paint and the termite infested black wood that barely kept the building intact. But inside of the bar was very classy. There was a live band and sometimes comedy shows during the weekdays. Due to the city inspector dropping by earlier in the evening, Big cleared the house. It was only him and a few of his goons around.

Tammy and Bow watched over Big's shoulder as he attempted the $1,000 corner bank shot during their game of pool. While Josh and Joey watched over the club, through tinted windows, Big threw the cube stick on the table, scooping his money in one quick motion. Tammy laughed at Bow then called him "sorry" as Big made his way to his desk, counting his money. She could never understand why Bow stayed in the game only to lose thousands of dollars to Big. Sometimes they would play for hours and hours, yet he would never win. Slowly, Big's office began clearing out, and all the chatter moved to the bar downstairs.

His mind wandered, thinking about the corner boy that was shot by the cop a week ago. Word on the streets was that the young man, an ex-dope boy, was on the path of straightening out his life. He was just in the wrong place at the wrong time. The cop on duty that day was going through a nasty divorce, and the pressures of his wife leaving him were what really caused the young man's demise, according to the public.

Big shook his head and grabbed his bottle of Hennessy from the bottom drawer of his desk. The young man worked for him a few years ago, but his parents gave Big hell! They called the police to bust up some of his corners due to fearing their son would spend a lifetime in jail, or worse, die. He only knew because Roper got wind of the young boy's parents calling the police and told Big he needed to let the boy go and to try to avoid bloodshed of the young man and his parents. Big smirked at the thought of him listening to Roper. He never thought the police would get their shot at the young man later in life. He could feel the sensation of the Hennessy overtaking his mind as he entertained thoughts and reminisced on him and Roper's last conversation. His drug-dealing coach's connections were way deeper than what he initially thought. He asked himself if Roper truly did keep him out of jail for all these years, and that he must know a lot more than he's leading people to think. He knew he even had a problem with the corner boy's parents.

Big started second-guessing, finding a new connect, in fear of how long Roper's hand truly reached. A new connect could mean hell raining down on his organization, but it was too late to change his mind. His next move could mean his freedom or death. The last thing he wanted was for his corpse to end up on the doctor's table and his organs shipped to the other side of the world, for profit. But it was too late! The decision had been made. The dope and money were already in play, and there was no way he could pull out of the deal now. Big shook his head in grief and began pouring another shot of Cognac. Roper 'suckered him in with that money' he thought, and now that he assumed he was dependable, he wanted to control him. He figured the only way out was to play ball and give them what they wanted. Precious lives in exchange for the almighty dollar. He took another sip from his glass and concluded he couldn't do it. He just didn't have it in him.

A knock on Big's opened office door snapped him out of his thoughts. As he motioned for Tammy to come in, he stared as she walked gracefully through his office. She was his right hand and conducted most of his business affairs. She was just as ruthless as Big and was the reason why bodies were dropping around the city. She was a woman in a dirty man's game and felt it necessary to play ten times harder and be one hundred percent tougher than her counterparts. Her power was respected, and her vengeance was feared around the city. When people didn't pay, it was a sign of disrespect to the whole organization. Also, for the poor souls that thought they could hide, she made sure they were found, and their corpses were in disarray and put on display for all to see their failed attempt. Big admired her enthusiasm and trusted most of her effective methods. Besides being female, she could move across the board like a queen in a chess game; unseen, but dangerous. He couldn't help but think that she may have taken things a little too far. With Roper on his back and no protection from the police, she made it ten times harder for them to move around. "Fuck it!" he thought as he took a long drag from his Backwood cigar, laced with gangsta's grass. There was no way in hell Roper could convince him to keep selling organs through the doctor. Besides, he was a hustler; not a butcher. He just didn't have the stomach for it. The first few bodies he sold made him sick the next day. He puked for hours and couldn't eat or sleep for weeks. Killing them was bad enough, but sending them to be butchered for spare parts on the black market was like gasoline in hell.

"What's wrong, baby? You look a little tense," said Tammy as she sat on the corner of Big's desk.

Her thick brown thigh dripped over the edge in perfect proportion, as she crossed her legs. Temptation peeked through her skintight dress. Big put his hand on her knee. Sexually, he was weak for a wet box he never had. This in return, never affected their business relationship. His tone with her was settled, but not tough. Even though she was ruthless, she was still a woman, and he treated her as such. He told her there would be no more killings without his permission. Big did not want to go into any details. He knew that if Tammy only knew she could eat from killing people, the whole city would be under siege. She and her goons would line Roper & the good doctor's pockets with souls. They wouldn't care if even the innocent ended up in the slaughterhouse. The thought alone made him cringe.

Tammy thought, "Damn! Is the boss going weak? What the fuck! Does he mean, stop killing?" Her eyebrows dropped as she stared coldly in Big's eyes while pulling a cigarette from her purse.

Picking up on her quiet demeanor and the way she sucked the cigarette down, half ash, let him know she didn't take the command lightly. Big patted her on the leg and said, "I need you here, not in some prison looking stupid, baby!" Big took another pull from his Backwood, as he dropped ashes on his $1000 t-shirt, carelessly.

After chastising her about her careless tactics, he explained their whole operation was about to change. The pick-ups and drops would be different. He also spoke about expanding their empire from state to state. He knew without protection from Roper that the streets would get hot, and change was desperately needed. Big did most of the talking, while Tammy sat quietly, listening, and smoking her cigarette. As far as she was concerned, Big wasn't thinking rationally. There were bags still owed, and a few of them required goons to ensure they cooperate or suffer. Putting out her cigarette, she grabbed her pocketbook hanging from her shoulders to retrieve a piece of gum.

Without any eye contact, she said with a little sarcasm, "I'm going to take Joey and Josh tonight to make a few cash pick-ups. If shit gets ugly, do we have your permission to shoot?"

Big noticed her mockery and just let her sarcasm go through one ear and out the other. She felt, to keep the streets under control, she would have to rule with an iron fist, which meant some people would have to die.

"Big knew this, just as well as anyone," she thought, as she half-heartedly listened to him go on about making the appropriate changes to his organization. His extravagant office and money made him lose sight of what was important. In the position they were in, weakness wasn't a luxury they could afford.

Big dusted the ashes from his shirt as he stood from his seat. He caught Tammy's eyes admiring his diamond cluster Rolex that danced with the light and the movement of his wrist. Ignoring her admiration, he poured another shot. There was a loud thump from the enormous glass desk as he set the bottle down. Relighting his blunt, he scrolled to the double tinted windows overlooking the bar.

He wondered if Tammy had obtained too much power. His absence from the street made her the face of the organization. Always using his intuition, he had seen her potential for betrayal, but he would never let it get that far. He thought while taking a sip of Cognac, if he had the (slightest notion of betrayal). He would make 'an appointment for her to visit the good doctor's operating table.' He would even have him prepare a special spot for her son she spoke of so fondly. He quickly dismissed the thoughts of butchering Tammy and her child after thinking of the loyalty she showed through the years. Besides, he was the one who made her a monster. It all started the day he put the first gun in her hand just so she could prove her loyalty. After hearing that she was kicked out of college for taking a guy's eye out with a fork when he touched her inappropriately, he prioritized making her a part of the organization. She returned home broke, with nowhere to go and a baby on the way. Although at the time he didn't realize she was pregnant, he had seen her struggles and loved her fiery personality. He took her underneath his wings, and she quickly stole his heart. With her extravagant beauty, her business savvy, and outspoken wit, she was tough like the guys and didn't take any shit. He was impressed by the way she handled herself and eventually became his right hand.

Sitting his glass on the window seal, Big leaned over, fixating his attention on the guys sitting at the bar. Tammy saw that his blunt needed to be ashed and took him the ashtray.

"That's what I love about her," he thought. When she saw that shit needed to get done, she handled it. Unlike the clowns at the bar: forever high or drunk.

Almost everyone has cleared out from the bar, except for Joey, Josh, and Bo. Joey and Josh were getting drunk while Bo stood behind the counter, playing bartender and peacekeeper. He was trying hard to calm Josh and Joey's constant arguing down before it led to bottle throwing.

"You see this shit, Tammy?!" Big said, staring at his drunken crew from the top floor in disgust. Now wishing she never brought the damn ashtray to him, Tammy said, sarcastically, "What boss? I don't see anything wrong?"

Knowing where his frustration was going, she thought, 'this was nothing new. Josh and Joey always fought. Hell, sometimes he would even instigate their fights.'

Pointing down at the bar and a little tipsy himself, Big said, "This shit!" noticing the trio, downstairs horse playing, "This is the shit I'm talking, about, Tammy!" said Big, clearly frustrated but keeping a calm demeanor.

Coldly staring into Tammy's eyes, he continued, "Shit around here, has to change!! From here on out, keep them niggas from getting fucked up on the job! That's number one, on the list. Y'all muthafuckers supposed to be my eyes and ears, and you are the only sober son of a bitch in the fucking bar, Tammy!"

Tammy silently smirked at the blind complement but remained quiet. She was a different person before her little cousin and uncle were murdered. She was outgoing with a bubbly personality and was crowned valedictorian and school president of her high school.

She lived in the country and had a pretty rough upbringing, but her family was okay. So, needless to say, when she heard her favorite uncle, who practically raised her, and cousin were both murdered, it was too much for her to bear. Her mind often slipped into dark places. Her little cousin, only ten years old, was robbed from the life ahead of her. She often thought that if she only knew their killers, she would make them wish they were never born.

They were never caught. Her heart hungered for closure, and she wasn't waiting on the police to do their jobs. To them, it was just another cold case. To her, it was her family lying on the living room floor both bleeding to death and holding each other until their last breath.

Noticing Tammy spacing out, Big passed her the ass end of the blunt to regain her attention. He explained again how much he needed her on board and how important it was for her to have their soldiers thinking clearly at all times.

Tammy thought 'mission impossible' as she dumped the roach in the ashtray but delivered a nod in agreement. Even though she remained quiet almost all through the conversation, the way she left Big's office said, 'attitude' all over it. Big knew she wouldn't take the news lightly, and it was obvious. Her thirst for power and blood consumed her. For Tammy, the money was great, but seeing paralyzing fear swallow a person entirely, was her real M.O. Big stared through the top deck windows, patiently waiting for Tammy to deliver his message to the drunken fellows at the bar. Big watch all three agree to his new plans. He observed Tammy not wasting any time, gathering Josh and Joey, to collect on his money. He called the bar downstairs from his cordless phone sitting on the desk and instructed Bo to pull the car around to the back.

The two crackheads hid behind an overfilled dumpster under a clear sky. The bloody moon was shining dimly, barely illuminating the poorly kept alley of the bar. The wind cut through their bones without remorse, but the dry freezing winds wouldn't keep them from their mission. The streets were deserted except for the cars that passed by. Once in a while

Henry rubbed his hands together, blowing in his palm, trying to keep warm from the blistering cold. Peering down the alley, he saw the headlights of the 95' Impala stopping at the side entrance of the bar.

"Just as Clyde planned," Henry thought. He clutched tightly to the snub nose 38 in his jacket pocket, waiting for Clyde to give him the signal to bring hell to the back of Big's bar.

Hearing the hammer cock back on the snub nose, Clyde quickly signaled for Henry to be quiet as he watched the man get out the Impala and enter the bar. This wasn't Clyde's first rodeo. At one point, he was one of the most feared guys in the city. However, his bad deeds caught up to a sleeping conscience, and prison temporally changed him. He experienced sleepless nights because of his victims' torturing him in his dreams night after night while serving his fifteen-year sentence for robbery and manslaughter. By the time he was finally released on parole, he tried to get a job and leave the streets alone. As a free man, life was a constant struggle. No one would hire an ex-con with a lengthy rap sheet the size of his. So all was left for him to do was petty crimes to feed his drug addiction. Clyde stole anything he could get his hands on. Once, he stole his landlord's refrigerator and sold it for $40 after being evicted for nonpayment.

Henry held the gun firmly behind his waist. He followed Clyde, crouching down. They moved quickly towards the door, positioning themselves for a possible ambush. Henry could hear his heartbeat through his chest. Petty crime and hustling were his M.O. Arm robbery and kidnapping were out of his league, but the thought of fifty grand made his hands sweat and his palms itch. This would be a game-changer for him, and the first thing he would do is get away from Brenda and her crazy ass kids. He smiled at the thought of freedom and anxiety was replaced with an eagerness to get the job done.

Henry thought his partner in crime, Clyde, had the entire job planned to a tee. He looked at the 95' Impala facing him, thinking he couldn't wait to get behind the wheel. He even fantasized about buying his own, after tonight's job was done. Quickly detouring from his fantasy, he focused on the chatter coming from the hallway. Clyde gave him a nod then signal for Henry to get ready. He slowly eased the 38 snub noses from behind his back. He could hear their chatter and footsteps slowly approaching the side door. He turned the 38 around in his hand, gripping nothing but cold steel. He knew after tonight that there would be no turning back and if things went accordingly, neither would he. As soon as the door opened, chaos broke loose as the butt of Henry's pistol came crashing down on Bo's forehead. One hard thrust cracked the wooden handle of the pistol. Blood gushed fiercely from Bo's wound as he collapsed to the ground. Clyde quickly burst into action, sucker-punching Big in the jaw and knocking him to the ground. He didn't waste any time snatching expensive jewelry off the necks and wrists of the dope boys while Henry held them at gunpoint.

Bo staring at the blood on his hands only pissed him off after his twenty-second nap on the concrete floor. Still dazed, he raised himself from the cold street, tackling Clyde to the ground. Henry stood in shock as he watched Clyde hit the ground. Minutes became seconds, and his dreams of being rich were slowly fading away.

"Ay, Ay! Get the fuck off him!" yelled Henry while still pointing his gun towards Big although his attention was solely focused on Bo.

Clyde's perfect plan was quickly becoming a shit storm, and it only got worse as Henry watched Bo reach for his waistline brandishing a 9mm.

Bang, bang, bang, bang! The sound of gunshots echoed through the dark alley. Silence filled the air as Henry's eyes gaped over Bo's lifeless body as it fell on Clyde. His stomach tightened, and the alley darkened. 'This wasn't part of the plan,' he thought. He heard Big jump to his feet to escape their raft.

"Henry!" Clyde yelled, "What the fuck are you doing? He's going, to get away!" pointing frantically towards the bar door at Big trying to get his balance to make a dash for it.

A sickness Henry never felt, filled his soul, and vomit rose to the brim of his throat. Even though Clyde yelled his name, regret held him stuck. This was his first time ever shooting anyone, and he never thought that popping his cherry would make him feel so miserable. Noticing the money man attempting to sprint away, Clyde quickly pushed the heavy corpse off of him and grabbed the gun from Bo's hand.

Bang!!! Clyde peered down the sights of the 9mm as smoke drifted from the barrel, as Big fell in the hallway entrance of the bar.

"Stop acting like a little bitch, nigga!" Clyde yelled as he witnessed Henry go through a mental break down, "And find something to tie this nigga up with!"

Henry was in too deep to turn back now. He swallowed his sickness and followed Clyde's instructions. After desperately searching through the bar, he managed to find duct tape and more cash after probing through a utility closet. They wrapped several rows of tape around Big's mouth, hands, and feet before throwing him in the trunk of the Impala. Henry swiftly jumped in the driver's seat while Clyde slammed the trunk. Pulling off slowly to avoid suspicion, they turned out of the alley, leaving the bar door open and Bo's body on the cold concrete to rot.

Having no idea how long they've been traveling, Big struggled to release himself from the restraints of the duct tape. Bo was dead, and the thought of him being next made him fight intensely for freedom.

Henry and Clyde celebrated their newfound success. While traveling down the dark country roads on their way to riches, Clyde skimmed through the jewelry and cash estimating their profits. Their laughter was loud as the two boasted about taking down the king of the city.

Boiling with anger, Big heard all they had to say. "Fuckin crackheads!" he thought, smelling the aroma of crack from the two celebrating their success. 'Bo usually kept a shotgun near the spare tire.' He hoped it was still there, as he continued struggling to free himself.

The road was empty, and nothing but agriculture stretched for miles. Henry let the window down to air the car out. Speaking loudly with excitement, Clyde told him that they would split eighty grand and still had another fifty a piece coming for Big's delivery. Bo's murder was light-years away and no longer on Henry's mind as he peered down at the jewelry and money from the robbery.

Dup, dup, dup coming from the trunk brought their pre-celebration and car to an abrupt halt on the side of the country road. Clyde grabbed Bo's gun from the glove compartment and put a bullet in the chamber. Without saying a word, he quickly stepped out of the car and headed towards the commotion. He signaled for Henry to pop the trunk with every intention of taking Big to his final destination; dead or alive. The trunk clicked halfway open, revealing the sawed-off shotgun at the other end. Clyde didn't see the fire coming from the barrel before his limp body was thrown 5' feet in the air from the gun blast. In distress, Henry searched his jacket pockets for the snub nose 38. Peering out the side-view mirror, he could see a dark figure holding a shotgun, closing distance. Giving up on all aspirations of a good old gunfight, Henry stomped the gas, leaving a dead Clyde and Big on the side of the country road.

The word "set up" hunted Big's mind like an angry hag as he dragged Clyde's thin corpse into the cornfield off the side of the road. He wiped the shotgun down with his now bloody $1000 shirt and laid it next to Clyde, then traded guns with him. Big was bleeding heavily from the side of his face. He felt his ear and flinched, noticing his lobe hanging by only a few threads of flesh. Using his undershirt, he applied pressure to his ear and focused on hitchhiking home. Big lucked up and found a payphone by a small deserted store. It seemed as if he had walked endless miles while applying pressure to his wound to control the bleeding. He searched his pockets for change and found $5 in quarters before reaching the payphone. He smiled at the thought of him having access to what he needed no matter where he was. Even being stuck in the middle of nowhere, he had a fist full of quarters. After $3 worth of pages, Roper finally called back. Thrilled he got Roper on the phone, Big explained to him that he was just robbed, kidnapped and shot. Roper was the last person he wanted to turn to for help, especially after their last conversation. Still, he figured Roper could help him clean the gruesome crime scene at the bar and maybe, have the Dr. sew his earlobe back on. Besides, it was a win, win for everyone. They get Bo's body, free of charge, and he gets his bar cleaned and ear patched up. Big was also curious to find out if Roper had anything to do with tonight's events. If so, Roper's hands reached further than what he could imagine and totally caught him off guard. It may have been in his best interest to leave things as they were and give them the corpses they wanted at least until he could find a way out from under Roper's thumb.

Roper's pager buzzed continuously. After several attempts to ignore the vibrations, he finally unearthed himself from underneath the two coked-up ladies. He was wondering who was draining the battery from his pager. He was just getting his night started, so he was reluctant to check the multiple pages requiring his attention. After hitting a few lines from the square glass mirror, Roper finally called the unfamiliar number followed by 911, from the suites' phone. His night was going well; he had two prostitutes on the top floor of a 5-star hotel suite. He had a bottle of champagne and almost half an ounce of coke. The ladies were high and didn't waste any time getting acquainted with each other. Things were going accordingly until his pager almost vibrated off the nightstand. The night was planned, but he wasn't prepared for the voice on the other end of the phone.

After hearing about Big's night, Roper's high was blown. It looked like someone was trying to beat him to the kill. That meant the flow of his money would stop before he could find a replacement.

'Mayor Ford would kill me; literally,' he thought, rushing to assist Big in any way possible.

A couple of hours went by before Roper's headlights brightened the small parking lot of the store. It was the best sight Big had seen in a long time, but still, the thought of someone setting him up wouldn't escape his mind. He was relieved to see Roper arrive alone but remained cautious as he entered the truck.

'He couldn't trust anyone, especially not this nigga,' he thought. Still, at the least he was grateful Roper showed up. Dying on a backcountry road is just not how he has seen it ending for him.

It was an eerie silence on the ride back to the city. Roper watched as Big wrapped fresh bandages around his head from a first-aid kit he had on the backseat floor of his truck. Roper retrieved a couple of painkillers he had in his glove compartment along with a few shooters of vodka he brought from the suite. Once Big finished doctoring on himself, Roper gave him both painkillers then shared a shot with him. The vodka broke the ice, and they began an open dialog with each other. To his surprise, Big had a sudden change of heart. He guessed a 'near-death experience' would do that to some people. After hearing Big's terrifying story, he was glad he called him first for help. A dead body at Big's bar was bad for business, so Roper didn't hesitate to call the doctor to clean up Big's nightmare. Roper knew there was hope when he finally got Big to see things his way.

"Do you know who did this to you?" Roper asked in a broad country accent, trying his best to sound concerned.

"Some fucking crackheads!! Clyde and…" Big snapped his fingers, trying to think of the other guy's name.

"Henry!" Big shouted out, recalling his annoying laughter. He told Roper one of them got away. The look he saw in Big's eyes gave him the chills. Before Big had the chance to entertain his thought, Roper quickly intervened, asking Big to let him take care of it. He could only hope this wasn't the same Henry he met during James's freshman year in high school. If it was, this could be a huge problem because he actually genuinely liked James. He saw a bright kid with a great future and didn't want Big having any parts in fucking up the young star's life.

Roper explained that he might know who this guy Henry was, but Clyde, he had 'never heard of.' Roper also told Big to let him take care of this fragile situation.

He figured he would show James's family more mercy than Big and if it was the same Henry affiliated with James, he would buy him a one-way plane ticket out of state, before he got himself killed.

Without putting up a challenge, Big simply agreed. Roper was right. If his crew killed the junkie, it could get ugly for James's family; especially with Tammy leading the troops. Besides, it wasn't him Roper had to be cautious of. It was the young niggas on the block that might think they were doing him a favor. Regardless of who was behind the trigger, Henry or Clyde's death would be satisfying to him.

Henry drove nonstop until he reached the next city. He found a bus station and a place to ditch the car and the gun about a mile down the road from a Greyhound station. 'Clyde's stupid ass plan nearly got both of them ,' he thought. He was speed walking through the small town holding his duffel bag full of jewelry and cash securely. When he arrived at the bus station, there was only a hand full of people sitting and lying around. He approached the counter and purchased a one-way ticket to Texas to live out his dreams.

CHAPTER 5
The Basement

The basement of Dr. Williams home resembled an autopsy room. There were red containers neatly stacked, forming a triangle on the hospital-like floor, along with several deep freezers that lined the wall. Centered perfectly in the middle of the floor were three metal tables that held at least two corpses each. There was also a large furnace built in the wall, like a fireplace, to burn useless tissues. Dr. Williams called this his 'office'; a place with an eerie illusion of an 'operating room.' The smell of stale blood and death's chills were heavy in the air. Big was amazed at how skilled the Doctor was, as he watched him diligently work on Clyde's corpse. He watched in disgust as the doctor carefully made a perfectly straight incision down Clyde's chest. Fresh blood drained from the cut streaming through the small holes on the stainless steel table. The sound of the bone saw carving through Clyde's ribs nearly forced yesterday's meal to the brim of Big's blunt stained lips.

Although it was the second time he swallowed his meal, his demeanor remained calm as he pointed to the body and asked, "Is that him?"

With no regard for human life, Dr. Williams smiled and quickly shook his head, nodding a "yes" in excitement.

"Do you guys want to see him?" he asked, eager to show them his new project.

Feeling yesterday's meal resurfacing, Big immediately declined his offer.

"Damn, that's Bo lying there!" Another piece of flesh for the black market, he thought, while trying not to stare at his friend's covered corpse on the table. Big started feeling guilty for depriving him of a proper burial; a traditional funeral with family and friends. Bo's heart and lungs would be sold around the world to the highest bidder. His flesh and bones would burn in what was referred to as the "hell furnace," leaving him to become a distant memory.

Roper first met Dr. Williams through Mayor Ford. Williams and Ford were fraternity brothers who pledged together in college, or as the Mayor would call it, "the good old days." Dr. Williams came from humble beginnings. His parents were the average middle-class family with big educational dreams for their son. They made sacrifices and scraped the bottom of buckets to make sure he received a good college education.

Even though the doctor's father's teachings remained branded in his heart, he slowly gravitated towards Ford's wicked energy. Ford was young and rich with no morals or conscience. He was known to force new pledges to drink beer with a mixture of urine until they vomited or passed out. He then forced them to eat their own vomit, and if they refused, it led to the possibility of being beaten to near death. Dr. Williams remembered an incident, while in college when he thought their new recruit would not survive the torture Ford was forcing him to go through. Ford seemed to be the one enjoying this the most. He had diligently studied his craft and was becoming a master at it. This young man may not have lived if Dr. Williams had not intervened, but his intervention caused him to become an outcast amongst his frat brothers. Worried about his life's goals going down the drain along with his parents' hard-earned cash, he decided it would be best to keep his distance from Ford, and just focused on his future. To Williams, this seemed to have been the best decision at that time. He was able to open up his medical practice in a low-income neighborhood, thinking it was a great accomplishment. Just starting out, his finances were low, and a practice amongst the big wigs in downtown Columbia was an unreachable dream. Although business was good and work was plenty due to high crime, and constant violence in the neighborhood, where the doctor had selected to open up his medical office. Eventually feeling overworked and overwhelmed, he started wasting his profits on alcohol and gambling.

His life was in disarray. He got involved with some of the wrong people due to his addiction to gambling, which also resulted to him owing more money than he had. The doctor was afraid for his life and avoided going to his office, fearing his debtors were there to collect what was owed this would cause him to lose more money and business. Things went from bad to worse when he discovered one of his nurses stealing from him. She was writing fraudulent prescriptions and selling them to addicts. He threatened to fire and report her if she didn't confess. She explained she was a single parent with three kids and needed the extra money for food and bills. His business was struggling, and he could only pay his staff minimal wages, which left the door opened for dishonesty and deceit. He wished things could be different, but after she confessed to whom she was selling the scripts and it being a lucrative business on the street, he felt he had no other choice but to fire her. He already had enough troubles of his own.

"The need for money can make you do desperate things," Dr. Williams thought to himself. 'He may have hit the jackpot? Could this be the way to pay off his gambling debt and unpaid bills?' Dr. Williams was back in business, this time by selling scripts himself. Greed would cause him to overlook common sense, and the D.E.A. eventually got wind of his scheming ways they busted his office and closed his doors. He wasn't in jail an hour before Ford, who was the chief of police at the time, pulled strings to get him released from custody.

The board snatched Williams' license, and he was no longer able to practice medicine. The doctor's back was against the wall. With no money coming in, he could barely afford to assist his sister with medical bills, his niece, who had developed rare liver disease. Her name was at the bottom of the donor's list, and he couldn't bear the thought of her dying. His house was in foreclosure, and the mounting bills for court and lawyer fees took a toll on his checking account. His niece was getting worse, and the hospital bills were becoming more than he and his sister could bear. Running out of time and options; he overheard a grieving family member of another patient mention they were taking their child to Mexico for a heart. Although it was highly illegal, and without any guarantees, he knew this was the only option for his niece. With little money left, he and his sister were able to scrape together just enough to fund a trip to Mexico, where his niece would get what she needed and make a miraculous recovery. Seeing the bright smile on her face again gave him hope and a brilliant idea for a new business venture.

Columbia was the perfect place to lounge his idea. Knowing about all the violence that went on by his old office building, he could make a killing profit with a business like this. His niece's expensive procedure was still a heavy burden on his life, and he needed to do something – anything that would give him access to easy money. He turned his fears into triumph once again by reaching out to his good friend Chief Ford, who was now running for Mayor. The Doc was not looking for a handout, but ready to discuss a proposition. If he was going to do this, he would need protection under the umbrella of the law. He knew his old college buddy would not pass on an opportunity to be part of a million-dollar operation. Dr. Williams was ready to put his skills back to work making his "profession" to organ trafficking.

While Dr. Williams carefully stitched Big's earlobe back on, Roper quietly slipped out the back door to use the phone in his truck. He called Mayor Ford to relay the good news. Now that Big was on board, there was no need to continue his orders of taking him out of his misery. Roper told Ford of the fresh body they had gotten for free and how much money they stood to lose if they got rid of their only money man so soon. Ford listened carefully but still wasn't convinced.

"Big's on the right track," Roper explained, still trying to convince the Mayor.

Ford was concerned that Big could be using Roper and would turn to his old ways as soon as he felt his situation was stabilized.

Roper entertained Ford's racist rants about Big but could not understand how he could hate someone he'd never met, so much. They made millions from Big and were about to make millions more; however, Ford didn't care. All he saw was color. He thought of rushing him off the phone before their conversation turned into a debate.

Roper thought if he hadn't convinced Ford to give Big a second chance, he didn't know how much more of his bullshit he would have been able to take. But despite the hatred because of his complexion, Big had a dollar sign stamped on his forehead, and he was the only person they had to move their product. Now that he was on board trafficking organs, their net worth would double. Roper felt a weight lifted off his shoulders! He was relieved he didn't have to kill Big, and business could go on as usual.

Dr. Williams finished stitching Big's ear and wrapped his head with fresh gauze. By the time Roper entered the basement, Big was ready to go. Even though it was the wee hours in the morning, the Doctor's job wasn't done. He rushed Roper and Big out of his home and grabbed a small saw from the tool drawer. He couldn't wait to start on Bo's corpse. Business was slow, corpses weren't coming in as expected, and the waiting list was at its highest. Most people looked at dead bodies in grief or disgust. To him, this was a work of art, and a corpse was his canvas. He didn't see it as taking advantage of a dead person but saving another human being's life.

James spent the entire month thinking of Grace. This particular day he felt joyful. He had not seen Henry in a few weeks, and it almost seemed as if his mom was becoming her old self again. He thought today was the day to make his move and get closer to Grace. He ditched his friends and went to Cora's Diner by himself, hoping his longtime friend and secret love would fall head over heels for him. On his way there, he thought of every word he wanted to say to her.

The cowbells rang on the restaurant's door as he walked in. Feeling a little nervous, but confident, James hoped he could convince Grace to go on a date. Somewhere they could avoid her father jumping out the bushes and catching them in the act of kissing. This was their senior year and a girl like Grace was for sure to leave this ratchet city to do great things with her life. This would be his last chance to tell her how he truly felt. 'It was now or never,' he thought.

Listening to her gracefully said, "Hello, James," and showing her white smile at the sight of him walking through the door, boosted his confidence. She continued waiting on customers, taking money from an elderly couple, and stuffing it in the cash register.

She was thrilled to see James and almost forgot to give the couple their change back. In a delicate voice, she apologized and handed them their change.

"Boy!! What are you doing here?" Grace asked with excitement.

The day was going better than he thought, noticing how gleeful she was to see him. After rehearsing his lines all day, he found himself at a loss for words once he and Grace were face to face.

James tried to find the right words to say, but he couldn't come up with anything other than..."I'm here for you, and your company outside of work. Do you think your pops will let you off early?"

With a genuinely sad expression and delightful smile, she said, "No, I can't... my dad won't let me. Business is really starting to pick up, and he needs my help more than ever, unfortunately, I may have to close tonight.

Here's my number, James. Maybe we can set our date for another time?"

James was disappointed but understood her dilemma. She jotted down her home number on a blank receipt, folding the small piece of paper before extending her number to James. That wasn't the answer he had hoped for, but he respected her decision. This was one of the many qualities she possessed beyond her beauty. Her loyalty and love for her family and friends made his heart melt. He thought to himself, "this is definitely marriage material." As he pulled the phone number from her hands, his fingertips softly rubbed her palm. They both met at the end of the wooden corner with open arms to give each other a tight hug.

James said jokingly whispering in Grace's ear, "Damn you smell like hamburgers and French fries." They both chuckled silently as they held on to each other, never wanting to let go.

The sound of Grace's father clearing his throat behind them startled them both. They quickly let go of each other. As Mo, Grace's father got closer to them, he stared into James's eyes, emotionless, and commanded Grace got back to work.

Compliant, she replied, "Yes sir," as she waved goodbye to James with a smile.

He put his pinky and thumb to his ear to signal he would call her later and after winking one eye in her direction. James rushed out the door before Mo had the opportunity to sit him down for a lecture about his daughter.

CHAPTER 6
Deception

Rper drove around the city with one knee under the steering wheel snorting mountains of cocaine from the creases of his fist. He had made Big's problem his own finding Henry, James's stepdad. What he didn't realize was that finding him would be so difficult. Weeks passed, and all of his resources led him back to one place, James's house. Wishfully thinking, he hoped for Henry's sake, that he had left the state or maybe even the country. He knew that if Big and his goons got to him first, the streets would be painted with his blood. Instead of riding past James's house like he has been doing for the last few weeks, he decided to check in on his family to see how they were holding up. As he approached the small shotgun house, he heard the kids playing in the living room with faint sounds of laughter. He rang the doorbell; and was surprised to see the small, fragile woman answer.

As he peered over her shoulder; he asked, "Is James's mother here?"

"Stop being silly, Coach! I'm Brenda, James's mom," Brenda said, greeting Roper with open arms and inviting him in her home.

Roper was surprised to see how much Brenda had changed within only a few years. He remembered when she was beautiful and living life, but now she looked like she had not had a decent meal in weeks. He knew James had it tough, but judging from the looks of his mother's condition, it seemed to be worse than he'd imagined. Crack totally destroyed their home. He was reminded of his childhood and felt remorse for James. After making small talk with Brenda for a while, he began to take a liking to her and the kids. Lord knows he had his vices, so being judgmental would be outright hypocritical.

She stated, with a straight face lying, that she didn't usually look so rough, but that the last few weeks without Henry had been tough on her and the kids. Her voice trembled, and her eyes watered when she mentioned that he had just left one night for no apparent reason.

"Oh! There was a reason!" Roper thought. 'That son of a bitch robbed Curtis, skipped town with the cash, he left this poor kid and his family here to pick up his loose ends. He was sure she knew more than what she was telling him and was only protecting Henry. Brenda insisted he had not contacted her or anyone they knew. Without a debate, he vaguely took her word for it. He didn't want her to feel she was under interrogation, so he switched topics and began asking her about James and some of the recommendation letters he'd sent to different colleges.

"This is one tough kid," he thought. Looking around James's house and noticing the extreme conditions in which he and his siblings lived. Roaches were crawling on the wall, and the box fan sitting in the window didn't blow enough air to keep the house cool, which made it muggy and more humid on the inside than it was outside. Roper had no intention of taking a seat after noticing the roaches. But once, he felt cocaine pouring from his pores because of the baking heat in the house, his head beginning to spin; he had no choice but to take a seat on the old worn out roach-infested furniture.

It was clear that Brenda needed help, and in a funny way, he felt he was responsible for their misery. It was time for Roper to go and continue his search, but before leaving, he offered to get Brenda some treatment at a rehabilitation center. He gave her his business card, which he usually gave to prostitutes and single mothers when he wanted to discuss their child's future with them. He reiterated how important it was for her to give him a call as soon as she heard from Henry.

Brenda happily accepted his card and noticed the few hundred dollars underneath, which made her day. No one had been this kind to her since James's father, and she definitely could use the money. In seconds of her holding the money under the cheap business card, crack infiltrated her mind like an infection. As bad as she wanted to change, she couldn't. This "snake" had its fangs buried deep in her arteries, pumping the venom through her infected heart.

With his hands behind his back and holding tight to a razor-sharp meat cleaver, Big paced back and forth on the concrete floor of the Bar's basement. He watched as Tammy marched twelve of his key soldiers through the cellar door to greet him and one of the local dope boys he had duct-taped to a chair. He was forty grand in the hole and had been ducking Big's goons for weeks. Big finally caught up with him the previous night, making him center stage for his horror show.

Everyone, including Tammy, was astonished to see the young dope boy's arms and legs duct-taped to a sturdy wooden chair. He was restrained so tightly the only body part he could move was his head. The legs of the chair slid from side to side on the plastic that was also duct-taped to the floor. As he struggled to free himself, Tammy and the entourage gathered around, silently observing saliva gushing from the bandana tied to his mouth. They ignored his cries and pleas as they echoed off the cellar walls.

Once everyone finished gathering around, Big made eye contact with the terrified dope boy. He put the dull side of the meat cleaver to his lips, signaling for the young man to hush. He didn't want anyone missing what he had to say. He waited weeks, giving his wound enough time to heal before he held this meeting. He didn't want to appear hurt like a wounded dog while demonstrating his power. Frowning on his crew of thirteen, he pointed the sharp cleaver towards them. There was a mole in his crew, and today he would find out WHO?

"You, come here!" said Big in a dull raspy voice, using the cleaver to summon Josh.

Confused and looking helpless, Josh glared at Tammy. His legs felt like rubber as he walked center stage to join Big. Everyone in the city knew Big was robbed.

"Why was he singled out?" Josh wondered as he stood in front of his boss like a disobedient child, afraid to face their parents.

Big played into the petrified atmosphere, pointing the cleaver to where he wanted Josh to stand. The kingpin of the city being robbed by someone in his crew and a couple of crackheads didn't look so good on his resume. If he had to pull every tooth in the basement, he was going to get to the truth.

Breaking the silence of Big's terrified audience, Tammy asked, "So Big… what is all this about?" referencing to the young dope boy, restrained in the chair, praying to the plastic beneath his feet.

Pointing the cleaver aggressively towards Tammy, Big replied, "That's a damn good question," patting one of the thug's shoulder and walking by each of them mean-mugging, peering through their souls.

"This nigga must think he is Scarface or some shit!!" Tammy thought to herself once he paused in front of her. "Here he is with this little nigga, tied the fuck up… waving the meat cleaver around like it's a magic wand or some shit. But, we, can't handle business on the streets without checking in first. Making us look weak as fuck He got me fucked up!" She laughed in her mind at the charades, but she couldn't say the same for the rest of the group.

Although they would never say it, or too tough to show it, every one of them was scared shitless. She saw it many times before; the different body gestures and facial expressions. The stench of fear seeped through their clothes like cologne on a musty body. After giving a speech about "loyalty" and 'biting the hand that feeds you,' Big instructed Josh to hold the dope boy's arm steady.

Urine streamed down the dope boy's legs, changing the color of his denim. He squinted his eyes and braced himself for impact. A loud shout from the basement door was the best sound the young man heard in years! Barely opening his eyes, he thought he saw the image of an angel whispering in Big's ear. Big listened closely to the goon giving him information about Clyde's old lady. Apparently, Clyde told her about the whole robbery; pillow talking her into a new life. After he never came home to drive her off in the sunset, she figured he probably skipped town with the money. His old lady got pissed and told all her smoking buddies that she was going to fuck him up if she ever saw him again.

Hearing the news, Big immediately shifted his focus by calling Joey and Tammy to meet him in the corner of the cellar. He gave them instructions to take the goon with them and to bring Clyde's girlfriend back alive. Quickly rushing them off, Big felt he was finally getting somewhere. He had a hunch who his mole or moles were, but he wanted to be certain before he just started killing people closest to him in his crew.

Besides the dope boy's sobs and the tapping of Tammy's high heels leaving the room, the basement remained pin-drop quiet. No one muttered a word as they listened to Big lecture them about loyalty while narrating his words with the meat cleaver. No one was leaving the basement until Tammy and Joey returned with the junkie. He didn't care if he had to talk all night. After a couple of hours of sitting around, Big jumped from his chair at the sound of the basement door opening up.

"What the fuck is this?" Big uttered, frustrated and pointing the cleaver at the trio. "Where the fuck is she?"

Noticing the other two were too yellow-bellied to say anything, Tammy took the lead and humbly said, "She didn't make…"

Fire exploded in Big's stomach, and the cleaver took a life of its own!! Anger fueled his strength, severing the dope boy's head clean off his body! Blood splattered and splashed through the room; mostly covering Josh's clothes.

Wiping the blood from his face, Big turned to Tammy, glowering at her as he cleaned the cleaver, with the bottom of his undershirt.

Not noticing Big coldly glaring in her direction, Tammy thought, "This nigga has lost it!" As she watched Josh vomit all over the severed head. If Big was looking for intimidation, his tactics were working perfectly. Most of the hardest guys in the room, including Tammy, had confused looks on their faces. No one could believe what they saw, but they all knew they didn't want to be next.

Smearing blood on her chin, Big forced Tammy to focus on him. His eyes were bloodshot red, and death pierced her soul, almost daring her to lie. He calmly asked her, 'what happened?'

She explained to Big that it was an 'accident.' Pulling him off to the side of the cellar, from the ears of the group, and she described Clyde's deceased girlfriend as being belligerent and loud. She explained the only reason "Sugar" talked was because Joey told her about him, and the mention of his name frightened her.

"She refused to leave the house, Big! And things took a wrong turn, man" Tammy said, recalling the events. "Her crazy ass ran to the kitchen to get a knife and threatened to stab your messenger," Tammy continued, being sarcastic.

"But she did tell us who your snake was before Joey was forced to shoot her ass!" she said, smiling like a sleaze bitch.

Full of enthusiasm, Big asked, "Who?" while holding the bloody cleaver out, looking for an answer.

"Josh!" Tammy said loud enough for the whole basement to hear and pointing at him as he cleaned the vomit mixed with blood from his face.

Shocked and confused, Big asked Tammy if she was sure. He had known Josh since Middle school and never had a loyalty problem with him. After a deep sigh, he signaled with his hands for Joey and the messenger to join them in the corner of the cellar. Big repeated the story Tammy gave him and then asked them both if the story was true. Without hesitation, both men agreed with her and peering at Josh, foreseeing his fate. Big couldn't understand! Josh!!Out of all people?! After all the shit he'd done for him, betrayal was the only thanks he had to offer?? Big was more hurt than angry at the notion of Josh's deceit, but that didn't stop him from leaving his corpse next to the headless dope boy duct-taped to the chair.

Earlier that day, Tammy did most of the talking on the drive to Clyde's girlfriend's house. She asked if any of them had seen or heard from Bo and why the hell were they looking for a mole in the crew when there were two junkies on the loose that robbed Big in the first place?! Why weren't they looking for them?? She warned them all, "we are walking on eggshells," and they could 'end up missing like Bo,' if they are not careful.

Pulling up to the one-bedroom shack, Tammy instructed Joey and the goon to stay in the car. Once she reached the house, Clyde's girlfriend met her at the door half-naked with only a polyester robe on, covering her thin frame.

She leaned on the door frame with a nasty attitude and asked the lady dressed like a detective or social worker, "Who the hell are you?"

Tammy politely introduced herself, then asked the polyester-wearing crack head for her name.

"My friends call me Sugar," she said, toning down her nasty attitude, trying to remember where she heard the name "Tammy." Realizing she was rude, she invited her into the house. Once Tammy was in the house, she didn't waste time drawing her pistol, backing "Sugar" in the corner of the wall, knocking down pictures. Sugar's eyes widened, remembering her and Clyde's conversation about a crazy bitch named Tammy, who wanted to avenge her little cousin's death, by robbing and killing Big. She fought with all her might, trying to evade Tammy but a gunshot to the chest killed her scuffle. Sugar laid on the floor gasping for air and pleading for her life, while shielding her face with her arms.

Tammy stood over Sugar, pulling the trigger multiple times until the gasping stopped. She muttered, "Stupid bitch," while cleaning off the pistol. She laid the gun next to Sugar's dead body, then walked out of the house like nothing ever happened.

As she entered the car, Joey yelled, "Tammy... What the fuck did you do?!!" Frantically putting the car in drive and peeling off.

"The Bitch was crazy man... I had to kill her!" Tammy said, lying through her pretty white teeth. She said, "Josh set Big up."

Joey looked at Tammy like she was full of shit.

"Josh?" thought Joey, "he would never do some shit like that; they went back since Middle school."

Once they were far away from the murder scene, Joey abruptly pulled the car in a gas station parking lot. He jumped out of the car and walked to the passenger side door. Yanking Tammy by the arm and pulled her out of the car. He demanded to know what she was up to and denounced, wanting anything to do with it. Their lives were on the line, and Tammy's chess game was getting dangerous. If they went back to Big's torture chamber with a half-ass excuse, all three of them could risk being checkmated.

After a few minutes of convincing Joey to see things her way, which she knew he would after the night they had and the things she did to him. He would bark like a dog if she made it make sense to him. After all, they were all underpaid. Plus, Big treated them like shit most of the time, anyway. She explained to Joey that Big was unstable, and if he didn't want to end up like Bo on the back of a milk carton, he should join her. By the time they reached the car, Joey was in, and after a few dollars, and a couple of life threats later, the young goon was onboard too.

CHAPTER 7
The Plot

Weeks passed, and no one had heard from Henry. To James, this was a blessing. The house was starting to quiet down with traffic, and his mom mentioned rehab to him a time or two. The only downside to it was that she would be gone throughout the night; most nights anyway, and he would be the one to watch his brother and sister. Never the less, the peace of mind was worth it. Most of the time, his siblings would be playing in their room or Grace's, and his friends would come over to keep him company.

Tonight, Brenda stayed in a little later than normal. 'Out of all nights!' James thought. He was doing all he could to rush her out of the house before Grace came over. He wanted her gone before she arrived. Not because he was ashamed of his mother, but because she and Grace would talk until it was time for her to leave.

It didn't look like he was going to get lucky tonight either, there was a loud knock coming from the metal screen door. It was one of his mom's friends delivering the news about what happened to Clyde's girlfriend, Sugar. She was barely through the front door and started blurting out the foreseen events. She told them word on the streets was that Big killed Sugar, Clyde, and Henry and she'd better be careful because her family could be next.

Looking back at James, Brenda rushed her friend outside. She didn't feel he needed to hear her antics. Besides, she'd heard from Henry already, and she vowed not to tell anyone. He promised to come back and get her and the kids once things cooled off. Finding out about Sugar's death was news to her. She felt she just might be next, but the crack was more powerful than death. As soon as her friend mentioned the "john" up the street, with a pocket full of money her focus shifted, and she yelled in the house to James that she 'would be back soon.'

James was delighted she was leaving. Finally, he would get some alone time with Grace to do the things he's been wanting to do to her for all these years. Thirty minutes passed. A soft knock on the door had James leaping off the old couch to see who it was. Grace had finally arrived. He'd prepared all day for this moment and had even sprayed on some of Henry's old cologne earlier and straightened up the house.

Grace noticed how clean the living room was and that James's clothes reeked of the old man's stench. She was impressed by what he had done for her, but things wouldn't go as planned for him. She wasn't there to bear gifts, but to convey the disappointing news. She told James her father liked him a lot but that for her safety, she couldn't come around anymore.

James sighed and muttered to himself, "Henry strikes again," sadly watching as Grace opened the passenger side door of her father's car.

Even though it was off-season, it was business as usual for Roper. Today was the day the monthly drop was kept underneath the backseat of his truck. He never met the person who made the drop. They just dropped the money in his 4X4 parked behind the stadium and moved on like nothing ever happened.

With all the drama surrounding Big, Roper didn't know who to trust. This particular night, he stood behind the bleachers of the arena, covered in the dark. The DEA's sister, Clyde's girlfriend, was found dead in her home a few days ago. There wasn't a doubt in his mind who pulled the trigger, and he felt it was time for him to have eyes on all players, especially the people dealing with him. He was surprised once he realized he had been spying on a tall, beautiful, black woman. He smoothly strolled across the parking lot and was happy when she stopped to smoke a cigarette. This gave him enough time to reach her and get acquainted.

"Hello, darling! I believe this is for me?" Roper said in a deep south accent, referring to the duffle bag in the truck.

"Only if you are the rightful owner," Tammy replied, flirting with Roper, not believing the guy in front of her was corny. She already knew his moves, after weeks of keeping surveillance on him, but she would've never guessed this clean-cut white boy with a karaoke singing personality, was this lame. She couldn't understand how a guy like Big could let a square like this control the operation. Although she didn't care, she followed the money, and this guy Roper was just another step up the food chain.

After a few minutes of standing around talking, Roper figured a couple of shots would open doors for them to get better acquainted.

Tammy gladly accepted Roper's offer for a few drinks and left her car parked behind the stadium. They drove for miles until they reached a redneck bar outside of the city. Before Roper took a drink, he was already "drunk" from her beauty. He played her sex appeal for weakness and figured she was cool. He was intrigued by her wit and classy personality. Before long, Roper was drunk and talked recklessly, mostly about stuff he had no business mentioning. The more shots of Tequila they downed, the harder it was for him to comprehend why Curtis didn't understand the more dead bodies there were in the streets, the more heat.

By the time Roper and Tammy parted ways, they were damn near partners in many ways. After years of Big knowing Roper, he had no idea Mayor Ford existed. It only took one drunken night and an eyeball full of cleavage for Tammy to have the blueprint on the whole operation. Now she understood why Big didn't want bodies in the streets and how Bo disappeared. She also noticed Roper wasn't too excited about Sugar's death; especially after he told Big that he would handle the situation. He explained to her that Big didn't know what kind of shit storm he started. He told her Sugar's sister worked for the D.A.'s office, and he was sure this wasn't a case they would sweep under the rug for the Mayor. He told her how he enjoyed coaching James because he was a special kid and nothing, but heartache would come to Big if James's family were ever touched or harmed.

Tammy and Roper danced until the early hours in the morning. This was the best night Roper had in a while and hated to see it end. He asked Tammy if she ever got high on her own supply while digging in his glove compartment and attempting to park at the same time behind the arena, next to Tammy's car.

"For a white boy, you OK, Roper," Tammy said, kissing Roper on the cheek, flashing her alluring smile. "But, I'll have to take you up on a rain check, sweetheart."

Tammy tried cocaine once or twice in college, and it wasn't something she was into. After her son's birth, she quit partying and began to focus. She winked her eye and swayed gracefully to her car. Roper glared lustfully as her backside bounce from right to left, walking away. She took one last glance, noticing Roper's look as if he was undressing her and blew him a kiss before entering her ride.

Brenda waited by the phone most of the day for Henry to call. She needed money for her and her babies to catch a bus out of Columbia. Sugar was murdered, and she didn't want to take chances with her kids. Big and his crew were ruthless, and she feared they would be caught in the crossfire if she stayed around. After a few hours passed, she realized Henry wasn't calling. She retrieved Roper's business card from her pocketbook and considered calling him for help. Brenda noticed James walking in the living room. He understood what his mom was going through as he secretly watched her hang around the phone waiting impatiently for what he figured was a call from that crack head boyfriend of hers.

"She's a fool if she thinks he's coming back," he thought. James had to be strong for his family. In a few months he would be leaving for college, but he vowed to get his family out this hell hole, no matter what it took. He was certainly not waiting around for some crack head on a white horse to do what needed to be done.

Brenda was proud of her son! He had come so far despite her own shortcomings. He had schools scouting him by the boatload; opportunities she never had. Her son had earned a free ride to any college he desired, and she wished his father was here to see him. Her consciousness weighed so heavy on her soul that she could no longer hide the dangerous situation Henry's selfish actions had put them in. She knew she had to be honest with James and asked him to take a seat on their old furniture.

Brenda thought her son had 'no idea what was going on.' Little did she know, his friends had already given him a heads up and told him everything they knew about Henry, Clyde, and Sugar. To make matters worse, she was completely unaware he had been walking around the house with a gun tucked in his trousers for weeks, vowing to protect himself and his family, no matter what the cost. The more Brenda spoke about how sorry she was and how Henry was coming back for them, the more frustrated James became. He figured she was probably doped up out of her mind and didn't know what she was talking about, anyway.

Weed smoke filled the presidential suite. Tammy's moans blended perfectly with the music in the background as Joey finessed her body. Gently kissing her neck and shoulders before roughly throwing her on the bed, he quickly unbuckled his trousers after throwing his shirt on the floor. He then slid his hands up her soft thighs and underneath her sundress. He proceeded to swiftly pull her G-string down, over her ankles, throwing them on the floor next to his shirt. She glared at him with submission in her eyes as he forced her on her stomach. She caught her breath once his rod entered her womb. There was a sweet sound of his torso pounding her perfectly shaped booty cheeks clapping loudly, and as he plunged his shaft in her wet box, it took him to another high!! Her legs shook, and her body quivered uncontrollably as she reached her climax. After finishing their 30-minute "workout," they laid in the bed exhausted, sharing a blunt.

For Tammy, everything was going as planned. She still wished Big was buried in dirt. She thought to feed him to the hogs would have been fun, but seeing him slowly drown in misery, was just as satisfying. Not even gratifying sex and sharing a blunt with Joey could deter her mind from making Big pay severely for her little cousin's death and his downfall was a damn good start. Besides, Roper wanted souls for money, and Big was too much of a pussy to give them to him. She knew she had what it took, and it was time to take over the whole empire.

She and Joey laid in bed, chuckling about how she played Roper! She couldn't believe he actually trusted her and told her everything. Big had it made with the police, politicians, and the Mayor in his pocket. She thought, "gold mine," as she passed the blunt to Joey. It was just one more nail she had to drive to seal Big's coffin.

It was only weeks before James and Grace would be leaving for college. James finally convinced her to sneak out of the house after weeks of professing his love for her. They agreed to meet in a park, not far from Grace's house. James wished he'd chosen a better day to link up with her. Just minutes before they entered the gazebo, the rain started to pour down, followed by thunder and lightning. For Grace, this was perfect, and even a little romantic. They sat close, keeping each other warm while discussing their future after college.

A roaring crack of thunder followed by a strike of lightning caused Grace to flinch. James took this opportunity to move closer to her wrapping his arm around her shoulder, giving her a sense of protection. While listening to the thunder roar, James asked Grace about God and why his life had to be so messed up. He figured she had some 'insight' since she went to church every Sunday. One thing they had in common was knowing how it felt to lose someone you love. Both had lost a parent at a young age.

When James looked into Grace's green eyes, the only thing he could see was her innocence. She responded to him by reciting Isaiah 43:2, *"When you walk through the water, I will be with you; and when you pass through the river, they will not sweep over you. When you walk through the fire, you will not be burned; the flames will not set you ablaze."* Hoping this would answer his question about God or bring him some comfort. Grace was truly full of grace, and James was amazed by her. He wondered how someone like her could come from a place like this with so much evil and darkness. Grace was beautiful on the outside and within. He was amazed at her ability to shine like a light, even in the darkest alleys of this corrupt place.

It had stopped raining for a while and time flew by quickly as they talked under the gazebo. Grace looked at her watch and noticed it was getting late. She had to be home before her father got back from his Thursday night revival. They embraced each other tightly as if this was the last time they would be in each other's presence. James slightly held Grace back as he gazed upon her beautiful face. Then, unexpectedly pulling her closer and sliding his tongue in her mouth, gently holding the back of her neck. He was truly enjoying every bit of her. The sweetness of her lips made it hard for him to let go. Watching as Grace walked away, James already started planning their next rendezvous before they had parted ways for college. As he walked home, he wondered if the park was the perfect place to meet next time. 'Maybe she would invite him to her house the next time her father had revival.' He smiled at the thought and quickly made his way home.

Tammy and Joey parked down the street from the worn-down crack house. They pulled up just in time to see James walking in his house. There was little to no traffic leaving their home, and with the rain starting to pick back up, they felt the timing couldn't be any better.

Once James got home, he noticed that his mom was a little more upbeat than normal. She had music playing in the background while she and the kids boxed up their belongings. She had reached out to Roper, and he agreed to help. She was concerned after Sugar's misfortune and needed to get out of the city, fearing she was next.

Roper promised a U-Haul would be outside her home the next day so she could start a new life giving her kids the future they deserved. Brenda had no idea Roper was already working on getting her a place in Atlanta so she could be closer to James when he moved for college. The deal going through just at the right time was just a coincidence, or maybe it was God giving her a second chance at life. She just so happened to call him that very same day, looking for help. After Brenda finished telling James about her amazing day, he smiled and blurting out, *"I will be with you,"* thinking of the bible verse Grace recited earlier. James thought, "Wow! There is a God." And rushed to his room to pack his things. Brenda looked at him confused, smiled, and waved him off to his room.

Joey put on a black ski mask and jogged slowly towards the small crack house. Halfway there, he put a bullet in the chamber of his gun. Creeping slowly towards the side of the house, he peeked through the window, noticing Brenda and the kids packing boxes.

Even though it wasn't hot outside, Joey could feel the sweat under his arm and forehead. This wasn't his first kill, but the thought of killing a woman and her kids made him feel a little uncomfortable, this was far out of his character.

Hearing Tammy's voice echoing in his ears and telling him he 'needed to do this to get to the next level' gave him the push he needed to do her dirty work. He took a deep sigh, knocked on the door and heard the voice of a little boy asking innocently, "Who is it?!"

Before receiving a response, James's little brother opened the door, allowing Joey to burst into the house. He closed the door behind him and grabbed James's little brother, holding him hostage.

"Everybody on the floor!!" He yelled while pointing the gun to the little boy's head.

Brenda started screaming from the bottom of her lungs, "Not my baby! Not my baby! Please!" She cried, running towards the gunman with her hands out.

Bang! Bang! Shots rang out, ripping bullets through Brenda's stomach and chest as she fell on the masked man, freeing her son from his grip.

James watched his mom as she fell on the masked man to her death. He jumped to his feet, attempting to escape to his room.

Bang!!! Joey fired at James, barely missing him, leaving a bullet hole in the wall.

Bang! Bang! The next two shots played on Joey's conscience before the bullets left the barrel. After, seeing the tiny babies fall on the dingy carpet, he asked himself, "What in the hell am I doing?" But it was too late to turn back now! Tammy promised, success and if he had to take a dark path, so be it!!

He quietly crept to the back room, looking for James before Joey could reach the hallway, James appeared from behind his door.

Bang! Bang! James fired two shots, missing Joey.

Listening to the exchange of gunfire, Tammy figured Joey was in a sticky situation. She checked her gun to make sure it was loaded, before rushing out the car to the rear entrance of the house.

James and Joey continued to exchange gunfire until there were no more bullets. Tammy entered the scene just in time to see the young quarterback wrestling Joey to the floor. She snuck through the back door and crept behind James as he was fighting for his life.

Bang!!! One shot to the back of the head and James's fight abruptly ended.

Tammy helped Joey off the floor, congratulating him on a job well done! Thinking the coast was clear, they suddenly heard low groans coming from behind them. Brenda was still alive!! She was struggling to breathe as she crawled on the floor, reaching out her hand to touch her babies one last time.

Bang! Bang! Tammy shot Brenda two more times in the back to ensure she was dead this time around.

Joey pulled his mask off and stared at the devastation that surrounded him. Looking at the children's lifeless bodies, just lying there, made him think of his own kids, who he rarely saw. His knees buckled with guilt, faintly hearing Tammy call his name.

"Joey!" Tammy yelled, trying to get him to snap out of his guilt trans. After a few seconds, Joey snapped back to reality, catching eye contact with the barrel of a 9mm.

Bang! Tammy put a bullet in Joey's head and watch his limped body fall to the floor next to Brenda's.

Feeling she was in the house too long, Tammy quickly wiped off the gun and laid it next to Joey. She then left out the back door, ran between the alley of the houses, opposite from the main street. She circled around the neighborhood, went back to her car, and watched as the crowd started gathering around, then she slowly pulled off with a satisfying smirk on her face.

CHAPTER 8
The Breakdown

The constant ringing of Roper's phone woke him out of his sleep. He leaned over to check the time.

"Shit!! It seven o'clock!" he mumbled, answering the phone.

"Hello,!" Roper said, frustrated, figuring a call this late couldn't be any good. For a few seconds, there was pure silence over the phone.

"Hello!?" Roper said again.

He listened in disbelief to Tammy on the other end of the phone saying she knew how close he and James were. She also said she was sorry to tell him some guy who worked for Big, murdered James and his family. Roper stared at his phone in silence. His stomach swallowed his heart. He could not believe Curtis would do something so stupid after he told him not to.

"Mayor Ford warned him," he thought, dumping a mountain of cocaine on the dimple of his fist.

"What happened?" Roper asked, sniffing loudly.

Tammy replied saying, 'she really didn't know.' She knew that Big was pretty pissed and she wouldn't put the murders past him especially after he'd killed Sugar, Josh and chopped off some poor kid's head who had nothing to do with anything.

Roper already knew about the headless stiff and Josh days after it happened. The money from the bodies had already been split two ways; between him and the Mayor. Roper had decided to keep Big's cut after finding out Sugar's sister worked for the D.A. After they cut all ties with him. Big's tough-guy routine had played itself out! They were just waiting for the right time to strike.

The phone beeped indicating there was someone on the other end. It was Ford, boasting and telling Roper, he told him so, coughing from the cigar he smoked. Then with a speck of empathy, he showed remorse for the boy's family. He asked Roper if he'd been to the hospital to see him yet.

"No!" Roper replied, "I thought he was dead?" Roper felt a small amount of relief to learn James was in critical condition. He rushed Ford off the phone and raced to the hospital.

Once he reached the waiting room, Grace's father stared at him as if he'd pulled the trigger, killing James's family himself. Roper tried ignoring his unpleasant stare, but they had to cross paths for him to reach the nurses' station.

Mo stepped in his path and said, "Don't bother! Everyone's been getting the same answers all night. They won't know anything until they're through operating."

Roper simply nodded and took a seat. After a few hours, people poured in from all over the city! Roper was surprised to see all the support James had as he watched a lady start a collection plate for the family's funeral and hospital fees. People filled the lobby with balloons and cards. He wondered about his own death…would anyone, other than Ford, show up?

Grace's father formed a prayer circle, those around held hands and bowed their heads. Roper joined the group, and as he stood there praying with his eyes closed, a tap on the shoulder interrupted him. It was Tammy! She was just what he needed; like a cold glass of water on a scorching hot day! Breaking mid-prayer, he sadly smiled and gave her a huge embrace. They both walked outside to share a cigarette. Roper felt pressure squeezing his heart, allowing it to cry its tears. He was outraged and couldn't hold it in, expressing to Tammy how much he wanted Big to die from the most gruesome death known to man!

Noticing Roper's passion for Big's death was equal to hers, made it a perfect opportunity for Tammy to volunteer her services, but she remained silent. She didn't want to appear bloodthirsty or rogue. She figured if he felt that boldly about it; he would initiate the conversation.

Tammy was right. Roper continued and asked 'just how close' she and Big were. She explained 'they were close but never lovers and she knew the business inside-out,' thanks to him. Her only problem with him, she said, was his 'sloppy work ethics.' She hated how he handled things and feared he would land them all in jail if he continued down his destructive path. Her face was as convincing as a car salesman's, and her words flowed better than a preacher. She told Roper she 'handled most of Big's business affairs but was harshly treated and underpaid.' She also went on to say 'she didn't even have money to pay a bond if she was caught up behind Big's insidious acts.' What she said next caught Roper by surprise! She asked! How much he would pay if she delivered Big to the doctor!? Roper smiled and thought he'd found his new mule! Roper groped her with his eyes and hands. She knew he wanted something more than just Big's dead body. She enjoyed his flirty ways but really had no intention of giving him anything more than eye candy. Roper was thrilled Tammy would go to the extreme for him, but he didn't give her a quick response. He liked her and thought she would be a great addition to his empire. It was just something about her he couldn't put his finger on.

"Big is your boss, but you're so enthusiastic about taking his life?! Where's the honor amongst thieves?" Roper asked, lighting up another cigarette, he caught eye contact with the chief of police. Roper excused himself momentarily, motioning for Tammy to take a seat on the bench by the double doors of the hospital.

"How sweet is that blackberry juice?" the Chief said jokingly, cracking a perverted smile.

Bored by the tasteless remark from the wrinkled face white chubby cop, he didn't bother shaking his hand.

"So, what's the update, Chief?" he asked.

He'd noticed a couple of his detectives talking to the doctor earlier and knew the Chief had all the information he needed.

Spitting tobacco from his mouth and grabbing his gun belt, the Chief said, "Yawls golden boy really dug himself a hole and if yawl not careful… you fellows just might get buried with him."

Patting Roper on the shoulder, he continued, "The masked man, found in the victim's house, was a known associate of Big. We're going to try to get him on the RICO Act, and the warrant will be issued in two days," the Chief said, spitting a slew of tobacco juice on the ground.

Roper watched as the slim of the tobacco dripped off his goatee. He thought, "disgusting" and pointed to where the leftover black residue resided on his lip, signaling to the Chief where he needed to wipe.

After wiping his lip with his index finger to clean the tobacco juice off with the seat of his pants, the Chief said, walking away, "Oh, oh!" snapping his fingers, "I almost forgot to tell you! Your star quarterback looks like he just might make it. He has brain damage, but with a little rehabilitation, he should be just like new."

Roper thought that was great news, walking towards Tammy, wanting to celebrate the good news with her company.

Smiling, as she watched Roper walked towards her, resembling a high school reject, she thought, "Damn it!! The little nigga made it," she assumed, judging by the goofy grin on his face.

She asked, "What was that about, baby?"

"James is going to pull through!! Isn't that great?" Roper said smiling and extending his arms out for her affection.

Embracing Roper, Tammy thought, "Yeah, great!!"

For Roper, the night was going great. His star quarterback was going to pull through, and Tammy just accepted his invitation to join him at his suite!

Tammy was surprised by how exotic Roper's penthouse was. Extravagant furniture with bizarre paintings lined the wall. She fell in love with the Steinway piano that sat by the window overlooking the city.

"You play?" Tammy asked. Rubbing her fingers across the keys of the huge piano, lightening her tone while envisioning a lifestyle she could see herself living.

"No," Roper said jokingly with a smirk. "The piano is only here to snort cocaine and fuck on. Besides looking good, it has no real purpose."

Tammy smiled at the response. Hell, she didn't know how to play either, but the thought of having sex on a grand piano moistened her.

Roper left Tammy in the living room to finish "creaming" over his furniture, while he fixed them a glass of his top-shelf champagne; not the cheap shit he drunk with the hookers. Tonight was a special occasion. He thought he would play some old school R&B and dim the lights. The music was a little too old for Tammy's taste, but she was feeling the atmosphere.

Roper slid next to her on the funny-shaped sofa, passing her a drink.

"Soo… Ms. Tammy, do you think you are ready to be Boss?" Roper asked, dumping a few lines of coke on the coffee table made of glass.

"No, you're the boss baby," Tammy replied, stroking his ego.

"I'm just the woman, that's going to hold your business together," She said, offering herself a little coke off the coffee table, playing into Roper's comfort zone.

"I don't think being Boss is necessarily a good thing being that you have a problem with authority," Roper said sarcastically, taking a line of coke up each nostril.

Tammy placed her liquor glass on the coffee table and faced Roper. With stern eye contact, she asked rhetorically if he knew the difference between a leader and a boss.

Drinking from his glass trying to maintain eye contact, he stared quietly, waiting for the answer.

She continued, "A boss is only in charge but a leader leads, teaches and makes people around him or her better," she said, picking up her glass, taking a sip.

She continued, "Big's no leader! He treats his people like footstools. We are overworked and underpaid!" Tammy took a swallow from her glass, finishing her drink.

"Shit, Roper! Big already killed three of his comrades; I'm not going to be the fourth!! I have a son to raise," Tammy said, leaning on the couch while taking off her overcoat to get more comfortable.

Roper couldn't believe how Tammy just fell in his lap. She was the answer to his prayers. All doubts of her he had was a thing of the past. Every time they met, their conversation was stimulating without sex, and that was something new for him. Roper explained she only had one day to get the job done before the police picked him up on a warrant. He made it very clear he didn't want him to make it to the holding cell. If she could do that, he promised her Big's position.

It felt like an eternity under Big's wing. Finally, she was getting somewhere. Tammy smiled at Roper raising her glass for a toast and said, "Consider the job done."

They both exchanged stories until the wee hours of the morning. Losing track of time, neither one of them could remember the last time they laughed into the morning hours. It was something new and different for both of them.

Tammy couldn't believe she was considering falling for a corny, country white boy, but he made her laugh. And it didn't hurt, he was going to make her rich.

Roper smiled at the thought of Ford losing his mind when he met her. Tammy was smart, witty, and the definition of a lady. He could see himself with a woman like her by his side. They both had the same ambitions and goals. She was the one he was waiting for.

When the alarm clock buzzed in Roper's bedroom, Tammy glanced at the clock on the wall. It was 8:00 in the morning. 'Where did time go,' she thought, gathering her things!

Holding up his index finger, trying to steal a few more minutes of her time, Roper rushed to his room to turn off the buzzing clock. He grabbed a small brown bottle from the nightstand to give to her. He figured if she was really going to do it, this would make the job much easier for her and cleaner.

Tammy was putting on her overcoat by the time Roper reached his dining room.

He handed her the bottle and said, "Happy hunting."

Confused, she asked, "What is this?" holding the bottle in the air.

"Oh… this?" Roper responded, retrieving the bottle from her hand. "This is just a little something the doctor gave me a few months ago… to help me sleep. If you can get close enough, drop a few dopes of this in his drink," Roper said, giving the bottle back to her.

"But not too much. I just want you to put him to sleep. This is the best way," Roper continued.

"It's quick, and it doesn't leave major organs damaged like bullets. We can lose a lot of money if too many organs are damaged… and make sure not to put too much of this!" Roper said, pointing to the bottle in her hand, "Because too much, may kill him!"

The word "kill" and looking at the bottle in Tammy's hand, made Roper's stomach twirl. He'd been Curtis's coach since the ninth grade. He taught him how to run a football and gave him his first brick. Plus the young man once saved his life. Killing him without answers just didn't feel right.

"I got to talk to him, Tammy, so don't pour too much of that, shit!" Roper said, feeling drunk and sympathetic.

"Hum"... You're talking like you've done this before, Coach?" Tammy said jokingly, taking the bottle from Roper's hand.

"Never," Roper replied, walking her to the door. He reminded Tammy that it had to be done sooner than later.

Tammy winked her eye, giving him a peck on the cheek and said, "I got you, baby."

Roper bit his bottom lip, watching Tammy walk towards the elevator. Not only did he like her; after their talk, he felt like he could relate to her. Ford wasn't the best person to work for neither, but at least the money was good.

Roper sat in the chair next to James's hospital bed. Still hung over from a long night with Tammy, he took a Tylenol and chased it with a cup of coffee, hoping it would cure his headache. It bothered Roper to see his star quarterback in such a terrible condition. James laid there lifeless with his head bandaged, and his eyes closed. If it wasn't for the heart monitor, you wouldn't know he was alive. Roper cringed at the notion of James almost making it out! The next day he and his family would've been on their way to Atlanta, starting a new life. Instead, the poor guy's family is dead, and he's stuck here fighting for his life! Roper wished he'd done something sooner. If only he gave Brenda money for a new place instead of a cheap business card, things may have been different. He wondered what James would do with his future now that he would never be able to attend college. He thought of taking him in just as Mayor Ford did for him when his father died.

Ford entered the decorated emergency room. Balloons and get well soon cards lined the table near the window from James's previous visitors.

"What a shame," Ford said, catching Roper in deep thought with his hands wrapped around his head, staring at the floor.

"Such great talent went to waste! What kind of animals would do this to a child?" Ford stated, adding his get-well card with the slew of others. Before Ford could get comfortable, Roper escorted him out of the emergency room, anticipating his bigotry. Besides, he couldn't wait to tell him that the "Big situation" was being taken care of, and his position was already filled by a beautiful young lady. The thought of a woman running his operation would send Ford through the hospital roof. Roper hadn't even told him she was black yet. He figured he would let him see that part for himself. He smiled at the thought of Ford really blowing the coop, once he saw her.

"Roper, what the hell... are you thinking, Son??A goddamn woman!?" Ford asked, rubbing the top of his forehead, trying to soak it all in.

"Sometimes I don't think you have the sense God gave a baboon's ass, Son!" Ford replied, trying his best to maintain his tone.

"Do you see that young man in there?" Ford said, pointing towards James, who was lying helpless in the hospital bed. "Please, don't let that be a young woman next." Before Roper could say anything else, Ford was knocking his shoulder out of the way, clearing a path for himself.

"Crazy old man," Roper thought, watching him walk down the corridor. He believed Tammy had what it took and if she could prove herself tonight, he would shut Ford's mouth once and for all.

It took nearly the whole day to track Big down. Tammy finally caught up with him in West Columbia, at one of his girlfriend's houses. It was a place where he could stash his money and clear his mind. He put a lot of ladies in homes, and she figured that out today by driving from one stash house to another. A lot of the young ladies he set up in homes ran off with his safe and left his houses empty once they got word of him being on the run for murder. After going through different names and addresses in a file cabinet in at Big's bar, she finally got the information she needed.

It was late afternoon, and the clouds already had buried the sun, radiating a red and pink skyline. Big peeked out the blinds of the mid-size house that sat in the cut. He was startled to see headlights flashing through the closed blinds. He grabbed his gun from underneath the cushion of the sofa, checking the clip and chamber to make sure that it was loaded. No one knew where he was; just the little chick he had living there. Big used her to run errands. She dropped off dope from his new connect to the few loyal friends he had left. He couldn't depend on many, but he labeled her solid. Still, in the crevice of his mind, his paranoia convinced him maybe she was followed, or she could be in on the take. Whatever it was, he wasn't taking any chances. His crew were dropping like flies, and if he could help it, he would not be next! Not giving the person a chance to get out of the car, he slung the door open, holding the pistol behind his back.

Big appeared distressed and down on his luck. He looked as if he hadn't had a haircut in weeks or a shower in days! The sight of him, bottom-feeding, made Tammy smile on the inside. She'd "tossed" a boss from being head of a team to him hiding from the police and tucking his tail.

"Checkmate bitch!" She thought, "He's getting exactly what he deserves," she concluded, thinking of her little cousin's death.

Hell flamed in Big's eyes as he watched Tammy walk towards the porch. Everybody was dying around him except for her crazy ass! She was still standing. Not to his surprise, she was a clever girl. He just didn't understand how the hell she found him all the way out here in the sticks.

Tammy gave Big a hug and a kiss on the cheek.

"You ok, nigga? You look like shit!" she said with sarcasm, holding in a cry out loud laugh but keeping her composure with a straight face.

Inviting herself in Big's mid-size home, she shoved a bottle of cognac in his hand.

"I'm Ok! Bitch! Where the hell you been?!" Big demanded, tucking his gun underneath the front of his shirt, shutting the door behind him.

"Is that any kind of way to talk to a woman that's about to save your ass?" Questioned Tammy, digging in her purse to give him the paperwork she found in Big's office.

"What's this?" Big asked, peering at the stack of papers in her hand.

"This... is how I found you!" Tammy said, staring at Big like he was the dumbest man on planet earth.

Pointing at the papers she held tightly, she said "Names, addresses, phone numbers... If the law got their hands on this, it would be a wrap for you... Baby! Better me than them," Tammy said, as she strolled through the living room taking a seat at the dining room table.

"Yea, you right," Big said, scanning Tammy's eyes, looking for the lying hole in her soul.

"They have been on my ass sis, ever since that bullshit happened with that crackhead bitch Sugar!" Big said, slightly letting his guard down. He sat the bottle of liquor on the table by Tammy and left to grab a couple of glasses from the kitchen cupboard and ice.

"Yeah, word on the streets is the crack head's sister works for the D.E.A," Tammy said, pouring them both a shot of cognac once Big sat the glasses on the table. She wanted to fall out of her seat with laughter! She never saw a nigga so black, turn so pale! Poor guy, Tammy thought. After all, the D.E.A wouldn't matter; she was the one sending him to meet his maker.

"Where's old girl?" Tammy asked, looking around the house for her.

"She's working overnight," Big said, leaving the table to take a piss.

"Look at this nigga," Tammy thought. She was watching him take his glass to the bathroom with him. 'After all the shit we've been through, he still doesn't trust me,' she thought, as she reached for the bottle of yak.

"Roper had said, a few drops?" Tammy thought rhetorically, opening the bottle of liquor on the table.

She took the small brown bottle from her pocketbook and listened for the toilet to flush. Discarding Roper's two-drop rule, she poured all the content from the small brown bottle in the cognac.

"Sooner than later," she thought, as she shook the bottle, and set it back on the table.

"Man! I'm not used to seeing you like this," said Tammy, reaching for the glass in Big's hand to pour him another shot of yak.

"Oh, it's not over for me!" Big said, ignoring her gesture snatching the bottle off the table to pour his own shot. Raising his glass in the air, he gave himself a lonely drunken toast.

"Oh yes, it is," Tammy thought, waiting on him to take his first and last sip. For a second, she wished she'd never agreed to tranquilizing Big like an animal. Once he began to speak about changing his life, God, black power, and all that righteous shit, she felt a little guilty.

Besides, who was she to play judge and jury on his life? Without him, she wouldn't be the woman she is now. She smiled to herself, thinking, "Maybe he taught her a little too well?" She turned up her glass pretending to take a sip and watching as Big drank the entire shot of poison, including the melted ice.

Feeling dizzy from the medication, Big sat his cup on the table.

"Bitch! What did you do to me??" he mumbled, fighting off the effects of the medicine.

Reaching in her pocketbook, Tammy pulled out the small brown bottle.

"I did this, BITCH!" she said, setting the bottle on the table.

"Why?" Big asked as he was slowly dozing off.

"You remember this lil girl, Nigga!??" Tammy asked as she slapped Big in his face showing him a picture of the innocent baby he slaughtered.

"That was my little cousin you killed in cold blood, coward ass nigga!!"

Big managed to muster enough energy to take the picture from Tammy's hand.

"I remember her," he mumbled. "She, she…" Big said, feeling the medicine kick in full gear.

"She what??" Tammy yelled, slapping Big in the face so hard the noise echoed off the walls.

Slightly snapping back to reality, Big stared at the photo again.

"Not me… that was Rope…." Big said before his arms fell in his lap, and head dropped to his chest.

CHAPTER 9
Heartless

Years ago, Roper coached an untamed Curtis sometimes weeks went by without him attending school. After being kicked off the football team, Curtis didn't feel the need to go anymore. Classes didn't pay for the small gold rope around his neck or the fresh pair of dope boy Nikes on his feet. His only interest in school was the cute females. Most days, he would hang out in the parking lot with Josh and Joey, waiting for the final bell to ring. They hustled nickel bags of weed to the kids on campus just to keep money in their pockets.

Coach Roper watched Curtis for years. He knew he was a troubled child and did his best to help straighten him out on the football field. He threatened to kick him off the team a few times but never did. Besides, the school council would go nuts if he didn't play. Even the time Curtis went to jail for a day or two, they insisted he starts in Friday's games until the news got involved. He had allegedly robbed some rich kids in the city of Lexington, even though he was never found guilty. The school had had enough and threw him off the team.

Roper knew the day would eventually come when Curtis would fuck his life up for good. He watched Curtis and his friends hustle weed for months in the parking lot after school and never said a word. He noticed his talents stretched further than the football field and saw an opportunity for both of them to live their dreams. "Curtis's life was already fucked up," Roper thought. "A motherless child... going nowhere too fast."

Chief Ford was about to begin his campaign for Mayor and felt all old ties needed to be cut. For Roper, this was great news! He hated dealing with the fat black dude they called Cowboy, from the Bishop Apartment Complex. He was loud and arrogant and wouldn't listen to shit unless the word came directly from the Chief.

He hated dealing with that prick! Cowboy was one of Ford's loyal snitches under his payroll, and Roper was only doing what he was told to do, which was pick the money up once a week from Cowboy. The problem was, he was never on time. He would have Roper waiting for hours then talk shit about the dope and his cut once he finally arrived! When Ford said it was time for him to make the cut, Roper thought, 'finally and he knew exactly who he would get to do the job.'

The air was bitter, and the heat barely worked in Roper's 88' Cutlass Supreme, but he drove past every corner until he found Curtis in the front of a store trapping weed.

"Get in the car, Son!" Roper said, letting his window down.

"Coach?" Curtis said, surprised to see any staff from the school in his neck of the woods.

"Yeah, Coach!" Roper replied.

"Get in!" he said, unlocking the door.

"Look, Coach! I don't want to hear that bullshit about me staying in school!" Curtis said, checking his surroundings for the rollers and jack boys.

"Mann! Get yo black ass in the car," Roper said, letting Curtis see a side of him he never saw.

"You got some weed?!" he asked, being persistent.

"Hell, yew!" Curtis replied, shocked that coach even smoked weed!

"Roll it up then, brother," Roper said, putting on his best black impression ever.

Without saying a word, Curtis held out his hand, wanting cash.

"He is exactly what I'm looking for," thought Roper, giving Curtis a hundred dollar bill for the nickel bag.

"This is too much, Coach," Curtis said. Trying to give him the money back out of respect. He didn't know if Coach was stupid or weird! Just that the whole situation felt awkward. He never thought he would be riding around the city, getting high with his high school coach.

"So, what's all this about, Coach?" Curtis asked, staring out the window at the broken city.

"It's' about you ruining your life and being some street punk on the corners! Selling nickel bags of this bullshit, won't get it!" Roper said, holding the weed sack in the air and showing it to Curtis, before putting it back in his pocket.

"You can look at me as a blessing because I'm here to change your life, Son!" Said Roper, turning in the housing project.

Wondering why the hell Coach was in the Bishop projects turning off his car and headlights, Curtis thought 'Coach was losing his damn mind.'

Continuing to pitch his proposition, Roper rhetorically asked Curtis how "successful" he wanted to become.

"I'm going to tell you something important. So I'm going to need you to follow me. Ok, Curtis?" Roper said, positioning himself to stare Curtis in his eyes. "Sometimes, in order to achieve the highest levels of success, you have to do things no one else is willing to do. That's the difference between an all American and a regular pro-player," Roper said, grabbing the 40 CAL from his waist.

"Aye!! What the fuck, Coach?!," Curtis said, reaching for the door.

"Calm down, Son!" Roper said, grabbing Curtis by the jacket.

"I'm offering you a "life" you only see in movies and read about in books! The shit, people dream about," he said, digging in his jacket pocket for the suppressor.

"Selling nickel bags of weed is not going to take you to the places I'm promising, Son! There's just one thing standing in your path to success; that loudmouth, fuckin' Cowboy!" explained Roper while screwing the suppressor to the end of the barrel.

"Cowboy?" Curtis asked, intrigued by the silencer. He'd never seen one outside of the movies!

"I know that guy."

"Well... that guy," Roper said, waving the gun towards Cowboy's apartment. "Is stopping you from becoming a very rich man. It's time to separate the boys from the men," Roper said, putting the cold compressor in Curtis's hand.

Shocked, Coach Roper was putting a gun in his hand, with a silencer attached, made him wonder, 'what was Coach was really involved in?!' Curtis sat there silently holding the cold steel in the palm of his hand. He could feel his heart beating through his black polo shirt. Although he sold drugs and did petty crimes, killing a man in cold blood was something new, but Roper was giving him a deal he couldn't refuse. A once in a lifetime opportunity to take over the city.

"Fuck Cowboy," he thought, feeling his anxiety diminish and mentally hyping himself to cause havoc in the Bishop.

"Are you ready to change your life?" Roper asked, full of enthusiasm.

"Hell yeah!" Curtis replied, opening the door to the Cutlass and following Roper to the worn-down apartment building.

It was no secret that Cowboy was known to have a lot of money. Curtis just couldn't figure out why the hell he chose to stay in the 'projects!'

"Just stupid!" he thought, shaking his head. Curtis watched as Roper knocked like the police on the metal door. The anxiety in his stomach slowly started easing to his chest, thinking his life would never be the same after tonight. But fuck it!! He was ready to casket this muthafucka if he had to.

It was a game night for Cowboy and his niece. Her father wasn't around, so on Fridays, he would take time from his busy night to spend quality time with her. It wasn't like he cared, anyway. He had niggas out there making money for him 24/7. The game was great, and Cowboy was "hood" rich. But for him, family was more important than the riches.

"I'ma show you how to play spades tonight Rayon," Cowboy said, getting the deck of cards from the kitchen drawer and throwing them on the table towards his niece. The loud knock at the front door startled him. He raced to the room, grabbing his gun from underneath his mattress in the bedroom.

"Who the fuck is it?" he yelled, holding the gun behind his back and looking through the peephole of his project door.

Roper shouted, "It's Roper!" signaling for Curtis to lean on the wall, out of sight. Roper figured Cowboy was holding and trying to avoid a gunfight; he wanted Curtis out of sight.

Cowboy opened the door, welcoming Roper in his house. He rarely stopped by, so Cowboy figured something was up with the package.

"What's up, Roper?" Cowboy said, putting his gun away. Without a response, Roper moved to the side, making room for Curtis to draw his pistol.

Cowboy yelled out, "What the fuck is this?!" while reaching for his gun he'd planted in his waistline.

"I wouldn't do that if I were you," Roper said, warning Cowboy that his draw wasn't 'faster than a bullet.' Calmly holding out his hand and asking for his gun.

Any other time, Cowboy would've said, 'fuck it,' and went to war. Yet, his niece was with him, and he didn't want to endanger her. He gave his pistol to Roper and complied to his demand to 'sit on the sofa.'

"I never knew you had such a beautiful daughter," Roper chuckled, tucking the pistol in his back beltline and escorting the little girl to the couch next to her uncle.

"I mean, a fat fuck like you, … she must take after her mother," he said jokingly.

"Fuck you, Roper! What the hell do you want?" Cowboy said boldly, holding his niece close to his side and staring at Curtis pointing the silencer in his face.

"What I want?" Roper continued, taunting Cowboy. "I want your money and the drugs you call "shit"… remember?" Roper said, putting all sarcasm aside.

"The dope ain't shit! And I ain't giving you shit, Bitch!" Cowboy yelled back, spitting on Roper's shoe.

Looking down at his shoe, Roper chuckled, surprised at the balls of Cowboy! Without hesitation, Roper said heartlessly, staring at Curtis, "Shoot the girl!" Pointing his finger at the baby on the sofa.

Glaring in the little girl's eyes, it was that moment when Curtis knew Roper had a few screws loose. He was already feeling fucked up for being in Cowboy's place on a promise that could turn out to be false hope! Plus, shooting a little girl was taking it to a place he wasn't mentally prepared to go.

"No! Please, no!" Cowboy begged, pleading with one hand and clenching to his niece with his other arm. "You can have whatever you want, just keep her out of it, Man!"

Without any remorse for human life, Roper shouted, "I said, shoot her!" Snatching the gun from Curtis, shooting Cowboy in the leg. The 40 CAL barely made a sound. As the bullet burst from the barrel, Cowboy screams filled the air. Watching him squirm and yell while holding his wound, excited Roper as he felt his nature beginning to rise. The feeling of being in full control of another person's life gave him power. It was a drug, and fear was the fire at the end of the stem.

Roper laughed out loud, mimicking Cowboy's cries for mercy as Rayon burst in tears, hugging nervously to her uncle's waist.

"Now that, was a warning, Boy! The next one will kill her," said Roper in a deep country accent, pointing the gun inches away from Rayon's spine.

Noticing the grimy smirk on Roper's face as he held the pistol to his baby girl, converted Cowboy's pain into rage. He vowed the first chance he got, he would shove Roper's revolting grin down his throat.

"It's in my bedroom closet," he mumbled.

"What did you say?" Roper asked, leaning in closer to hear what he was saying.

Moving his niece out of harm's way, Cowboy lunged from the couch, punching Roper in his jaw and knocking him to the floor!

Surprised by the sucker punch, Roper dropped his pistol! He frantically tried to retrieve the gun from the white plastic tile while trying his best to ignore the powerful blows to his face that drew blood from his nose and mouth. Roper felt himself fading away with each strike, but the fear of death and survival kept him reaching for the butt of his pistol.

"Clink, clink, clink!" Three shots to Cowboy's back saved Roper from being knocked unconscious!

Feeling dizzy from the fatal punches, he pushed Cowboy's lifeless body off of him!

"Go check the room for that money!" Roper griped, ashamed and embarrassed. He stood up and brushed himself off while staring at the little girl in front of him. Her watery eyes told her story as she glared at Roper while kneeling on the floor and holding her uncle in her arms. She groaned, and tears poured from her eyes.

"Hurry up!" Roper yelled out to Curtis, annoyed by the little girl's cries and pleads for help!

Curtis had never seen so much money and drugs in his life. The shoeboxes were full of the Fifties, Hundreds, and lots of dope! He smiled as he laid the gun in the box with the coke and rushed back to the living room. The sight of Roper standing over Cowboy's dead body quickly brought his joy to a complete stand still.

Before Curtis could think about what he'd done, Roper said, "That's a lot of shit there, huh, Boy?" reaching for the shoeboxes. After checking both boxes, Roper smiled 'deviously,' taking the gun from the box with the coke in it.

"Shoot her," he said coldly, holding the gun by the compressor screwed to the end of the barrel.

"No!" Curtis declared, refusing to take the gun.

"She's just a little girl, Man!"

"Yeah! A little girl that can point us out in a line-up!! Now, take the gun and kill that little bitch!" Roper demanded, shoving the pistol in Curtis's chest.

"Hell, no!" Curtis protested, slapping the gun away from him. "I'm not going to shoot some innocent little girl… are you crazy??!"

"Why not? You already shot her daddy!" Roper replied with a grin, reminding Curtis of what he'd just done.

Noticing Curtis standing firm in his decision, Roper pointed the gun in his direction and stared down at Curtis, looking for the slightest ounce of fear. To his surprise, there wasn't any. The kid was as cool as a cucumber, and Roper knew at that moment, he made the right choice. Silent bullets whispered from the gun, hitting the baby girl twice in the chest. Her tiny body fell onto her uncle's torso.

Curtis couldn't believe what he just witnessed!

"Coach is a fuckin, maniac," he thought, watching Roper unscrew the compressor off the gun and stuffing it in his pocket.

"Did you touch anything?" Roper asked.

"No!"

"Good!" he said, giving Curtis both shoe boxes.

"This is yours, Son!!You deserve it tonight. Now, let's get the fuck out of here!"

After a quiet ride through the midnight air miles away from the crime scene, Roper pulled over on the river bank and turned off the headlights and engine. Curtis was overzealous with the shoeboxes full of money and coke he held in his lap, but couldn't help but to feel nervous once the car lights went out. Roper was as unpredictable as life itself, especially after witnessing him murder that little girl in cold blood. He wasn't sure Roper could be trusted. "But fuck it," he thought. "Roper held his end of the bargain so far, and if he could make it through the night, his life just might change forever! Besides, he saved his life when Cowboy was beating the life out of him."

"Curtis!" Roper yelled out, standing at the edge of the riverbank, "Come here!"

"Here we go," thought Curtis putting the shoebox in the backseat. "Showtime," he mumbled.

Closing the door of the 88' Cutlass, Curtis noticed Roper toying with one of the guns. "Shit!" he thought, stopping halfway to the river bank, as his legs muscle stiffened.

"What's up, Coach?!" Curtis asked.

"Come here!" Roper said while wiping the gun down with his undershirt. "It's alright, Son."

Once Curtis reached the river bank, he observed Roper breaking down the pistol piece by piece. "Tonight never happened... you understand??" said Roper, spreading parts of the pistol throughout the Congaree River.

"I know the game, Coach!"

"I know you do son, that's why I chose you to help me tonight."

"So all that cash… is mine?"

"Yes, but the coke we split 60/40." Without giving Curtis a chance to respond, Roper continued,

"You did good tonight, Son… so it's only right, I keep my end of the bargain… after all; a deal is a deal… Right?"

"Roper…?" Tammy pondered, trying to figure out the connection between him and her uncle. She looked at Big slouched out in the seat with his head down, drooling on his tee shirt and no longer breathing. She grabbed the picture of her little cousin from his hand, which was already starting to stiffen with rigor mortis and stuffed it in her pocketbook.

"Wow, Roper …?" She mumbled.

Tammy gathered the ashtray, empty glasses, and the bottle of liquor from the oak wood table. She cleaned her lipstick and fingerprints from them. She then dumped the ashtray and put the shot glasses back in the cabinet like they were never used. Then, she wiped the Hennessy bottle and threw it in the trash can along with the collection of others.

Everything was going as planned, despite the fact Roper asked her to bring Big back alive; that was never part of her plan. Big was going to die; with or without Roper's help! She'd been planning Big's demise for years! Roper just played a very small part in her show; and mysteriously, he just made the lead role. At least she knew what she was dealing with. Roper was a snake that needed his head chopped off, and she felt she was the perfect person for the job!

Once Tammy made it to the nearest pay phone, she placed a call to Roper.

"It's done," she said, whispering in the phone as if someone was listening.

"Great… What's the address? I'll send my guys out right away."

After giving Roper the location, Tammy took a deep sigh, "I got some bad news, Roper."

"Fuck, Tammy! What is it?" Roper griped.

"Our guest didn't make it."

"What? Fuck! I'm on the way!!"

After an hour and a half of just sitting around and watching Big's corpse rot, a white van pulled up in front of the mid-size house. Two guys got out of the van with white hazmat suits and fishnets over their heads. They wiped everything over, including the wood grain floor! They even took the trash. Not long after they started working, Roper arrived. Although he was pissed with Tammy's lack of ability to follow specific directions, he was glad the whole Big situation was said and done. He grabbed a pair of shoe covers and gloves from the van before he entered the house.

"What the fuck happened here, Tammy?!" Roper asked, not knowing whether he wanted to kiss her or smack her.

Pulling the last cigarette from the box in her purse, Tammy pulled off an award-winning performance. Her hands shook as she lit her Newport 100.

"Everything was moving so damn fast! I really didn't have time to think or to measure the dosage, Roper," Tammy explained.

"I'm sorry! You know, it's not like I do this type of shit all the time!! Right??" she continued, burying her head in Roper's chest as she forced a few tears to screen down her face. She took a quiet sniff and continued with her guilt trip.

"I'm sorry for crying, but he was like a mentor to me, and I killed him for you," she sobbed, looking up at him so he could see her watery brown eyes.

Diving head first in her pity pool, Roper hugged her and patted Tammy on the back.

"You didn't do this for me. You did it for us, sweetheart," he said while drying the tears from her cheek with his thumb. He glared in her glossy brown eyes, letting her know they were in it together.

The zipper from the body bag interrupted his moment of condolence as he watched the two men in hazmat uniforms prepare to load Big's body in the van.

"Oh, yeah! Once you're done with that smoke, make sure you put that cigarette butt back in your purse. It's some new shit that's out to help detectives solve cases called DNA. The slightest bit of your saliva on that cigarette butt can land your pretty little ass in prison for a long time. Besides I'm sure ten years down the line, you wouldn't want to go down behind this shit."

"Yeah, I guess, your right," replied Tammy, putting the Newport out with her fingers, she placed the short in her purse and asking Roper, "So I guess, he's off to the doctor, Huh?

"Yeah… I reckon, so," Roper sighed, watching the men load Big's corpse on the cargo van.

Tammy smirked, "That dude probably haven't seen a doctor since one smacked him on the ass!"

"You just might be right."

They both laughed while getting in their cars and leaving the crime scene.

CHAPTER 10
Lost

It had been months since Henry checked in with Brenda. He moved from one roach hotel to another, thinking the police or even worse Big, and his guys were after him. He'd smoked and spent most of his money on junkie hookers that indulged in the same activities as him. He only had seven thousand dollars and jewelry left from the robbery. His dough was starting to decrease, so he started thinking it was in his best interest to move back to South Carolina before he found himself homeless in Texas.

After several attempts of trying to reach Brenda, but only getting a dial tone, Henry became frustrated and threw the hotel's phone on the floor. He thought, 'She was finally done with all his games and found some other dope boy to fulfill her desires.'

The more the idea danced around in his head, the more upset he became. 'After all I've done for her and them damn kids,' he thought. "I can't believe she would do this to me!" He mumbled "Bitch!", where only the walls could hear.

Henry sat on the bed and wondered if moving back to Columbia was such a 'good' idea. Only if he could contact her, he would be able to find out if it was safe for him to return home.

"Fuck it!" He sighed, picking up the phone to call the dope man.

"Aye this Henry! You got a hundred, man?"

"Yeah… what room you in, nigga? The dope boy said, recognizing Henry for being a big spender.

"Room 507 at the Crown Inn." An hour passed before there was a knock at the door. Henry had been waiting anxiously for his routine morning high. So, when he heard a muffled thump, he ecstatically leapt from his queen size bed to answer.

"Who is it?!" Yelled Henry, excited his package had finally arrived.

"It's Zo... Open up!" The drug dealer answered in a raspy voice. His white tee and blue jeans were sharply creased, matching his shining white Nikes. Stepping in the door, he looked around the room in disgust. The small one-bedroom looked as if a hoarder resided in it. Empty food containers, bottles, and empty crack vials covered the floor.

The hotel room reeked of crack and musk, as he held his tee shirt over his nose, he said, "Open up the door or something! It fucking stinks in here, my nigga!" Griped the dope boy, frantically digging in his pockets for Henry's drug of choice.

Ignoring the drug dealer's request, Henry peeled off a hundred-dollar bill from the wad of money in his hand. "Fuck that! Do you want this money, or not?" Henry said, wide-eyed and jittery, feeling a pre-high from the crack being in his presence.

The dope boy's eyes widen with greed at the sight of Henry's stash. It didn't matter to him how Henry accumulated the bankroll; he just knew he wanted it.

The hundred dollars he initially came for, was chump change, compared to what his beady eyes were set on.

Henry sensed the little punk scamming on his bread and stuffed the wad of hundreds and fifties back in his pocket, but still holding firmly to his C-note.

"Shit, man! I think I left that shit in the car bro," the dope boy said humbly.

"Don't fuck with me, boy!" Henry snapped.

"Ain't nobody fucking with you, nigga. I'll be right back!" The young man insisted, shutting the door behind him.

Henry could smell the con in the air and for a second, he wished he never ditched his gun. His gut feeling told him the little nigga was up to no good. Yet, his desires outweighed his common sense! He ignored his gut and hoped for the best. This time there was no knock at the door. The dope boy busted in the room, brandishing a pistol, aiming it straight between Henry's eyes!

"What the hell is this?!" Henry shouted, throwing both his hands in the air and cussing at himself for letting his habit overthrow his better judgment! He hesitated, retrieving the money from his pocket. It was his last, and he feared, if he were robbed, he would no longer be able to support his addiction or afford his room. The pistol crashing down on the side of his face helped him to make his decision quickly.

"You Mothafucka!" He yelled, quickly retrieving the wad from his pocket. He felt blood trickle down his cheek, falling on his dingy, wrinkled shirt.

"You know what time it is!" The dope boy said smiling, showing a mouth full of gold and holding out his hand, wanting all the junkie's money. The Dope boy's eye dimmed the shiny yellow gold, stuffed in his gums, as he pressed the barrel of the gun to Henry's forehead. Even though the money was already in his pocket, the thought of killing Henry haunted the young man's trigger finger as he softly tapped the trigger.

"Kill me, Kill me! I don't give a fuck, nigga!" Henry yelled, like he had nothing to lose. "You got everything I have nigga!" He proclaimed, holding his gushing wound.

The dope boy gave him a long cold stare as if he was trying to read Henry's lying soul before he dashed out the room to make a clean getaway.

Henry didn't bother giving a chase. He simply propped his arm on the frame of the door and silently kicked himself in the ass! Watching the dope boy sprint through the parking lot to his car.

"Mothafucka!" He said, holding his wound and slamming the door behind him. Lucky for him, he stashed the jewelry! He figured he could at least get a few grand for the Diamond cluster necklace. Not to mention, the rings and watches he jacked from Big and his goon. The seven thousand was a huge loss, but at least he had his life and a way out! He gathered his jewels and sat them on the dingy bed sheets. He grabbed the watch then stashed away the rest of the jewelry. He hoped he could get at least three or four grand for the Rolex.

The hotel parking lot was nearly empty. A cool breeze blew the daily paper over the cracked concrete. The sun shined, but the air had a bitter chill. Henry held the watch tightly inside his coat pocket, shielding his hand from the cold air as he darted to the pawn shop. Henry was almost out of the parking lot when he heard a female yell his name from the balcony of the hotel.

"Henry! Where do you think you're going handsome?!" Shouted the smacked-out white girl. She was wearing nothing but Daisy Dukes, a bra resembling a shirt with the cheapest raccoon fur the flea market had to offer!

Her skin was pale with sores over her arms where she constantly picked and scratched.

"What do you want, Beth? I ain't got time for your shit today!" said Henry, not breaking stride in his walk, assuming she only wanted a free high.

Racing down the stairs, she joined Henry. "So, what happened to you today? Judging by that awful bruise and Zo running from your room, it looks like you've been robbed. I told you not to fuck with that nigga, but…"

Quickly cutting her off, Henry replied, "Minding your business, Beth, it's the freest thing in this world!"

"Well, it's everyone's business now. I heard you got rob for seven grand," Beth replied.

Braking his stride, he stopped and turned towards Beth. "Where the hell did you hear that from?"

"Nigga, please! I'm a bitch with ears. I hear everything! So, where are you headed to now that you're broke?"

"Oh! You didn't hear? I'm far from broke baby, that bullshit was a minor setback!"

The pale-faced white girl smiled and locked arms with Henry then said, "So, where are we going, daddy?"

It felt good having a woman under his arms again. Even though she was nothing but a heroin shooting hooker he had gotten fully acquainted with over the last few months, she invited other women to their rendezvous and he would purchase the "smack" to make the nights perfect. He often thought of trying heroin, but knew it was out of his league. Tonight may be different, he thought, holding the skinny white girl under his arm as they walked to the pawnshop.

The cashier in the pawnshop immediately recognized something off with the couple, as he watched them enter the shop with a graceful stumble.

"If yawl in here to sell stolen shit, get!" He yelled, standing in arms reach of the double-barrel Winchester.

Henry lifted his hands in the air and said, "Mannn… ain't nobody here to steal from you or sell you stolen shit! I'm here to do fair business, brother."

The cashier stared at the hooker in disgust and said, "You can't fool me, boy! That thieving bitch tried to clip me once! For now on, I leave my wallet home and only take forty dollars for that slut's nightstand. She steals everything, boy!" The once pale man started turning beet red at the thought of her trying to pick-pocket his days' worth of wages after sex and depicted both of them to be thieves!

Henry regretted ever letting the conniving whore latch to his arm for their journey! He stared at the cashier in his eyes, taking the focus from her and demanded, "Look, man! I don't know what she's done to you, but my shit's legit! Just let me take a moment from your time and let's talk business, man!" He said as he walked closer to the red-faced cashier. Gradually watching his demeanor change, Henry approached him on the far end of the counter.

"How much can I get for this?" Henry asked, taking the clustered Rolex from his pocket. Surprised from the clear clusters shining on the watch, the cashier took a step back before retrieving the Rolex from Henry's hand.

"Wow, boy! Where did you steal this nice piece of equipment from?" he said, as he stared at the watch dangling from his fingertips.

"Look, man! I told you, I ain't no thief!" Henry said, snatching his timepiece from the cashier's hand.

"Ay baby! Let's get the fuck out of here!" He demanded, stuffing his watch in his pocket and grabbing the white girl by the arm, forcing her towards the door.

"Wait, wait, wait!" Henry heard as he made his way to the exit.

"What, man?!" He snapped, turning around to face the cashier, "What can you possibly want from a thief?!"

"You people can't take a joke to save your life, can you?" The cashier said smiling, showing every yellow tooth in his mouth.

Offended by the comment, Henry sucked in his pride and answered, "What do you want, man?" Seeing the geezer's eyes light like a Christmas tree after he'd seen the rainbow clusters in the watch, he knew he had him bagged and tagged! His inside smile reflected his walk to the counter. "So, what is it, man? Are we going to do business or what?" Henry said, slamming his Rolex on the table.

Staring at the Rolex, the cashier sucked his teeth and said, "We can do business, but I can only give you $1,500 for the watch."

"$1,500!" Henry shouted, pushing his unorthodox negotiating skills to the max.

"$1,500 is all I can do," said the cashier pushing the watch towards Henry, "Take it or leave it."

With a pocket full of cash, a pistol tucked in his trousers, from the deal he made with the cashier, Henry and the junkie stopped at the corner store, and bought two grape Mad Dog 20/20's, a hundred dollars' worth of crack, and heroin from one of the corner boys who was standing in front of the store. Even though $1,500 wasn't nearly the amount of money he hoped for, at least he'd found someone to buy the rest of the jewelry without getting himself robbed in the process of selling it. The dope stuffed in Henry's pocket caused their bodies to fiend as they rushed to his filthy hotel to get high. Once in the room, the skinny, malnourished junky, didn't waste any time throwing her raccoon fur on the bed, making herself comfortable. The spaghetti straps from her shirt exposed the tracks left by the brutal bites of the needle. The pint-sized purse she held contained all the utensils she needed to begin her journey. Henry eagerly watched as she retrieved the large elastic band from her pocketbook, then placing it next to the bent C-shaped handle of the spoon on the table.

"If I didn't know no better Henry, that look in your eyes tells me you're just as curious as George," she said, reaching for the brown powder bag in his hand.

"I don't know about George, but I am feeling the urge to have a little taste of that."

"A taste of what... me or the "Dog food?" She said flirtatiously, referring to the heroin she was pouring in the spoon.

Giving a slight smile, Henry replied, "Both!"

She chuckled, then filled the bent spoon with water, after putting a small amount of heroin in the spoon.

"Hold this, baby," she said softly and struck a lighter, burning the bottom of the spoon.

Henry watched as the flames boiled the water in the spoon turning it brown. His bald forehead started to sweat. Butterflies flew around the edge of his stomach with anticipation as she dipped the syringe in the spoon, draining the brown water from it. She laid the syringe on the small round table and picked up the elastic band lying next to it. She then wrapped it tightly around Henry's skinny arm until a nice ripe vein appeared. After plucking the syringe a few times to remove the air bubbles, she slowly eased the tip of the needle in the middle of his vein, ejecting the poison in his bloodstream. Extreme heat cloaked his body, and the butterflies he once felt became moths! His eyes rolled in the back of his skull as he felt the devil's venom in the pit of his stomach, giving him the best high he ever felt.

Beth watched as Henry puked over his already dingy shirt. "Fucking amateur," she mumbled, carefully digging in his pockets for the cash, trying to avoid getting thrown up on her hands. She found the wad of money and stuffed it in her tiny purse along with her utensils, leftover crack, and heroin. She then scanned the room, looking for more valuables. She stumbled across a duffle bag lying on the corner floor of the closet. Her uncontrollable excitement nearly made her burst out in glee once she opened it, but she kept her composure and silently left Henry's room.

After several minutes of enjoying the best high he'd ever experienced, Henry woke up dazed to a lonely room. He immediately checked his pockets to discover that all his cash and dope was gone. Rage took over as he flipped over the small table and stumbled to the closet. What he saw next, destroyed his high! His duffle bag was missing, and he had no cash.

"Fucking Bitch!", he yelled, storming out the room just in time to see her and her pimp vacating the premises.

"Mothafucka … where do you think you going with my shit!" Henry yelled as he raced towards the smacked-out pimp, knocking him across the head with the butt of his gun. The pimp fell hard on the patio's concrete, groaning softly while holding the growing knot on his forehead. The prostitute gasped for air at the sight of her bruised pimp holding his injury. She tried making a dash for the stairs before Henry caught her, but it was too late!

"Bitch, did you think you could steal from me?" he snapped, pressing the gun to the back of her blond skull, then checking her pockets for the cash she stole.

"I'm sorry, I'm so sorry!" she pleaded, holding her hands in the air and dropping the duffle bag on the patio. Henry's rage died down at the sound of the jewelry clinging in the duffle bag once it hit the patio's pavement, and the feel of his sweet cash returning to the palm of his hand caused him to practice trigger control.

"Bitch! You lucky I don't kill you now!" he whispered in her ear, tucking his pistol in his trousers.

But the shove to Henry's back knocked him into Beth, sending her headfirst off the balcony! Her yells were sudden and short once her body hit the pavement below. Both Henry and the pimp stared in fear as they watched blood ooze from the side of her temple.

Without thinking, Henry picked up his duffle bag and ran down the hotel's stairs. A half a mile from the room, he watched as sirens rapidly passed him. He put his head down and started walking, picking up the pace while looking for a safe location to hide in the wide alleys that didn't seem to provide any cover. He ran until he ran out of breath! Pausing to take a deep breath, he put his hands on his bended knees, and remembered when life was much simpler selling dope in Columbia. With every breath, he saw it all coming to an end as he spotted another police car fly by. He figured his odds of evading jail would be greater if he got out of town.

Just a quarter-mile from the bus station, his fast-beating heart nearly stopped when an officer slowed down catching eye contact with him. His legs became rubber bands, buckling at the sight of the officer getting out of his car. It was all but over when the cop drew his weapon, forcing him to the ground. The barks of, "get on the ground!" forced him to comply along with the gun pointed to his forehead. Once on the ground in cuffs, the cop started stumping and kicking him repeatedly asking him if he really thought he could get away with killing a white girl.

After nearly breaking Henry's rib cage, battered and bruised, the cop threw his weak body inside the back of the patrol car and hauled him off to jail.

CHAPTER 11
New Beginnings

nce James opened his fatigued eyes, he scanned through every smiling face in the room. He had hoped to see his mother in the crowd. His face was full of confusion blended with pain, that sharply traveled through his head. Flinching from the infliction he suffered, James touched the bandage wrapped tightly to his head.

Grace was the first to embrace him. She'd been praying for this moment for several months and was relieved God had answered her prayers! Tears of excitement moistened her cheek. She delayed going to college, despite her father advising her different. She explained to him that James didn't have anyone and she wanted to be one of the first faces he saw, once he woke from his coma. Even though Mo hated the idea of Grace starting school late, there was nothing he could do. Her mind was made up and him fussing would just perpetuate the problem.

"What happened?" James mumbled, noticing the sorrow in Grace's eyes. She knew this moment would come the second James opened his eyes. Her heart wasn't prepared to be the bearer of bad news. She looked back to Roper for assistance, only to see his joy become short-lived. He let go of Tammy's hand as he squeezed through Killa Man and Crazy Cory. The doctor warned him of James suffering memory loss. He felt it may be too soon to drop such a heavy load on the young man's shoulders, all at once. Feeling his sorrow, Roper suggested James get some sleep.

"No… no, Coach! Tell me what the hell is going on," James protested, letting out a faint cough.

"Where in the fuck is my family?" Tears brewed in the bottom of James's eyelids before Roper could deliver the horrible news.

Staring at Roper while he calmly broke the news to James, Tammy reflected on how she felt losing her uncle and cousin. Even though she contributed to James's misery, she couldn't bear the sight of watching the young man break down. Without causing a scene, she quietly grabbed her pocketbook and slipped out of the room. As soon as she entered the hallway, she heard a cry of anguish that only a broken heart could produce. James's screams echoed down the corridor. The more he yelled, the quicker she walked, trying to escape the harsh reality she'd created. There was no remorse after she killed her victims, but listening to James mourn, was not in her playbook.

"I'm not about to listen to that bullshit," she thought, pushing open the double doors to the hospital.

The air was brisk and slightly windy, forcing Tammy to shield the Bic's flame to light her cigarette. She took a long drag from the cigarette thinking how much her life changed over the last few months. Roper came through with his promise, and she had the world at her fingertips! She would never have had this life had she still been working under Big. She was in the process of purchasing her own condo and buying her first car. Every car she drove was Big's.

He would only feed them enough to make them come back for more. Even the house she lived in was leased through some chick that worked for Big. She finally understood how it felt to be the boss. But, there was just one thing she found hard to get over; Roper's name being mentioned in Big's final breath. The money, the lifestyle, none of it mattered, if it was true that Roper participated in the murder of her family. She figured, she would enjoy the sweet perks of spending his money while saving hers and plan the perfect time to strike. Once she was able to maintain her lavish lifestyle, 'he wouldn't even see it coming,' she thought, flicking her cigarette to the ground.

The hospital room was quiet after James cried all he could cry. The sounds of the heart monitor beeping to the rhythm seemed to pass time.

"Man, this shit is fucked up…Coach!" Crazy Cory said, with all 250 pounds of muscle aggressively approaching Roper.

Roper looked confused. He was lost and really didn't have a clue why Cory was trying to live up to his name. "Boy, whatever on your mind, I would strongly suggest you leave that shit in your neighborhood," Roper said, staring at Crazy Cory shrinking his size. "Now, if something is wrong… Son, we are going to talk about it like gentlemen and not fight. We're not some thugs on the street!" Roper said.

"What's wrong is that grimy ass bitch you brought with you!" Crazy Cory said, lowering his voice.

"Who, Tammy?" Roper asked.

"Yea, that pshyco bitch! This nigga, from my hood, said she was the one that killed Sugar and might have killed my cousin Big! No one has heard or seen him in months! That bitch is crazy, Coach, I'm telling you," Cory responded.

"I don't believe you!" Roper said nonchalantly as if he forgot the foundation on which their relationship was built.

Crazy Cory, still trying to convince him, said, "Look, Coach! This man has no reason to lie…" Roper glanced around the room, and it seemed like everyone agreed with Cory, everyone except himself and James. He was dozing off from the morphine the nurse pumped in his vein to calm him down, after his outburst.

"What exactly did the young man say, Cory?" Roper asked, making sure his name wasn't part of the testimony.

"He said he was there and saw it all! From that crazy bitch shooting Sugar to her and some other nigga, named Joey making him say that Josh set Big up to get robbed. He believed she killed Sugar so that the truth wouldn't get out!"

"About what?" Roper asked, clearly becoming a little frustrated.

"Damn Coach! Aren't you the main person that preaches to us about being sharp and aware?" Cory said, with a little sarcasm, as he continued, "Tammy, Coach, she was the one that set Big up in the first place. Don't you get it?? She might have had James…"

The tapping of Tammy's high heels brought the room to complete silence. Her presence was like a pitch-black cloud in the sky, that didn't produce one raindrop, but you knew, after the first one fell that all hell would break loose! The last-few-months Roper spent with Tammy were amazing! Together they were dropping twice the units and making twice the cash. She had the streets mapped out to a science. She eventually extended a lot of business to the country, which turned out to be more profitable than Roper could have imagined. The Mayor was happy, and even the doctor was happy. It turned out, Big's body parts paid more money than any of them anticipated.

The allegations brought against Tammy were substantial. With Roper being seen parading her around, he knew it wasn't a good look for his image, and neither was this fucking kid, playing news reporter. He could mean bad news for her, and that would mean bad news for him. He didn't know how far the gossip traveled. He just knew the head of the snake, needed to be chopped off, before he hissed in the wrong person's ear about Tammy's horrific acts.

On the ride back to Tammy's condo, Roper zipped through traffic, jumping from lane to lane, aggressively moving freely through cars. He just conquered one problem; now here he was faced with another. There was no way in hell he could go to Ford with this dilemma. This one, he figured, he'll 'handle on his own.'

No sooner than the elevator dinged to the pent house suite of the condo, Tammy asked, "So what was that all about, at the hospital?"

"Nothing you have to worry your pretty little mind about gorgeous," Roper answered, staring at Tammy's tall, dark, perfectly shaped figure as she laid her keys and purse on the kitchen counter.

Even though she knew he was hiding something, she took his word with a grain of salt and simply said, "Ok." She maneuvered through the boxes she had yet to unpack, to slip into something more comfortable.

"Well ... there is something I would like to ask you, Tammy."

"Well, spit it out, man, damn!" Tammy shouted from the room, throwing on a halter top and jogging pants.

Roper felt stupid and played - she had him hooked! He had given her the world and all he received in return, were lies. He didn't realize how little he knew about her. Looking at her pocketbook sitting on the kitchen countertop, without giving it a second guess, Roper opened her purse, not sure of what he would find.

"Why didn't you tell me about, Sugar?" Roper shouted, peeking around the corner to make sure the coast was clear. It didn't take a lot of rambling through before he saw a picture of a little girl smiling, full of life, the life he took with one squeeze of a trigger. On the back of the photo, it read, "To my favorite cousin in the whole world, Tammy." Roper couldn't believe his eyes, as he put the picture back in her pocketbook. Listening her footsteps moving closer to the kitchen, he pretended to unload the boxes.

"You mean, the D.A.'s sister right?" she said, helping him unpack.

Even though Roper had a direct line to her bullshit, he played it calm and continued to help her.

"Yeah, her," he said.

"What about her?" Tammy asked.

"Let me start by saying, in order for us to maintain a healthy relationship, trust is key. I can trust you, right, Tammy??" Roper asked, handing her an empty glass to store.

Tammy sucked her teeth and responded, "What do YOU think Roper? Haven't I proven my loyalty to you??"

"Your loyalty to our business is not in question; unfortunately, your acts are, Tammy. Now, I need you to tell me exactly what happened with Sugar," Roper said in a stern voice, trying to be patient.

"Sugar's dead, Roper! What in the hell else you want me to say?!" She said, sassily raising her voice.

"How about starting with the truth?!" Roper snapped back.

The tension in the air was thick like fog. The penthouse was so quiet, you could hear a fly's conversation. For the first time, Tammy was stuck with no other angle but the truth. She grabbed Roper by the hand and led him to the displaced loveseat in the den. Once Roper took a seat, she began.

"I had an uncle, his name was Mike, better known as Cowboy," she sighed. "He moved here from the country and brought me with him when I was only thirteen. I never knew my dad... Let's just say on the weekends, after a few bottles of Mad dog 20/20, I became a punching bag for my mom. My environment was toxic, and it seemed like he was the only person that gave a damn! After moving here, he enrolled me in school and made sure I was taken care of. He even paid my college tuition. My uncle, Cowboy, was a good man."

Wiping a tear from her eye, she continued, "He was also in the process of getting custody of my little cousin. She was going through a similar situation, you know?" More tears fell from Tammy's eyes. She got up from the love seat to retrieve a napkin and a cigarette from her pocketbook in the kitchen.

"This cross burner been through my shit," she thought, noticing that the photo in her purse was out of place. She kept her thoughts to herself, lit her cigarette, and joined Roper on the loveseat.

"So, you were mentioning ... what was his name? Cowboy? That's it!" Roper said, snapping his finger to his own answer.

"Yeah, Cowboy!" She said, nodding her head. Her soul shook in rage, hearing Roper speak of her uncle's name. 'How could this piece of shit even look me in the eyes,' she thought.

"The Devil himself! A fucking snake!! Damn, him!!! I'll take this cigarette and burn a hole through your fucking blue eyes,' Tammy thought but shared the end of her cigarette instead of acting on impulse. She figured it was better to be kind to him right now because that would make her revenge that much sweeter. Pulling herself out of the sunken place, she forced a half-ass smile and continued her story.

"Big fuckin' killed them... he and his fucked-up friends killed them both!! So see, that's why they all had to die! You believe me, don't you Roper??" She looked at Roper with her big, brown, coconut eyes and uncrossed her curvy thighs. Roper had never seen this look in Tammy's eyes before; grief mixed with an erotic passion for sex. When she licked her bottom lip, he felt his manhood bulge in his underwear.

"You believe me, don't you baby?" Tammy seductively said, putting her hand on his knee, slowly moving it towards his nature.

"I, I..."

Before he had a chance to respond, Tammy's tongue was massaging his. He closed his eyes and felt her ecstasy reach every crevice of his body. She erotically moaned while unbuckling his trousers. Roper began kissing her neck slowly while taking off her joggers. Her skin was so soft; it seemed to melt in his mouth and hands. He gripped a palm full of her ass and leveled her body on the love seat. Her warm, brown, thick thighs vice-gripped his back, forcing his manhood to enter her warm, tight womb. Harmonious moans filled the entire condo as Roper's staff slid in and out of her. The wetter she became, the more difficult it was for him to fight his explosion, coming uncontrollably in her vagina.

Panting hard, struggling to catch his breath, Roper said, "Wow! That was great, beautiful," attempting to run his fingers through her hair, but she quickly moved her head away.

"Is anything wrong?" Roper asked, putting his trousers back on and feeling like he was nothing more than a petty fuck.

"No, it's just…" She said, trying to respond.

He gently placed his finger over her lips and said, "Shh… You no longer have to worry, I'm here."

'She never felt so disgusted,' she thought, wanting to laugh out loud, but instead smiled gently and excused herself to the restroom to scrub Roper's scent off of her body.

The googly look in his eyes made her feel those five minutes of anguish, were all but worth it. She had him right where she wanted him, and in due time, she would be the one doing the fucking.

All the gossip Roper heard about Tammy tonight, ceased to exist. Her truth mixed with her sweet ass heightened his admiration for her. She single-handedly brought Big to his knees then slit his throat when he was too weak to walk.

"Crazy, but fucking hot," he thought.

Watching her walk in the den, he figured having her on his team was a blessing, but also a curse! The only good thing about the scenario was the only person that knew the truth had his body parts spread out across the world, for profit. So, as long as she believed Big and his guys killed her beloved uncle, she posed no immediate threat to him, but he still wasn't out the water yet; there was still the Sugar situation.

While Tammy unloaded boxes, Roper poured a healthy line of cocaine from his vial on the marble countertop. Sniffing the whole line of white powder, he said, "This lady, Sugar, can become a problem for you, Tammy."

"How? What the fuck are you talking about, Roper?" Tammy asked with a little irritation in her voice.

"What I am telling you Tammy-you don't get it, do ya? You fucking made a mistake! Some dude you took with you to kill Sugar is running around, running his yap, saying he was there when you killed her," Roper sniffed, catching the cocaine's snot running from his nose, as he continued his sentence. "This is a big problem and it could be bad for business."

"So we take him to see the doctor, no big deal, right?" suggested Tammy, taking a seat next to Roper.

"No, sweetheart, it's not that simple. The information was given to me by one of my students, and if this guy mysteriously comes up missing, I could be implemented," Roper explained.

"And that's exactly why we should have the doctor clear another table; no bodies no crime, right? Problem solved," joked Tammy.

Though she said it in a joking way, Roper didn't find it funny. In fact, he found it to be outright disrespectful, once he thought about it. He loved those kids! They were good, respectable kids when they played for him. He did everything he could as a coach and mentor, to set them up for the best life possible. He even went as far as having Mayor Ford write recommendation letters. The redneck was reluctant in the beginning. He said, "This would tarnish my good image if one of those niggas got out there and fucked up." But, Roper convinced him that doing this little act of kindness could be a good thing, by possibly increasing voters in the black community in large numbers. Just from the letters alone, and at the least it made a great sound bite.

"Do me a favor, Tammy and shut your fucking mouth! Don't you... EVER talk about my kids in that manner!" demanded Roper.

"So how do you suggest we handle the problem?" Tammy asked sarcastically.

"After a few days, I'll let you know," Roper said, still irritated, rising from the loveseat and kissing her on the cheek, before he left.

There was a nice crowd in Club Bananas, and the music burst through the speakers playing "Gangsta Party" by Tupac. Juju sat at the bar and indulged in drinks. He'd been at the club for most of the night and found himself tipsy from the double shots he was throwing down back to back. He lied for Tammy to save his own hide, resulting in an innocent man's death. That didn't bother him. The fact that people were disappearing without a trace first Bo, then Big, had not only him but also the streets in disarray.

Tammy terrified him! No one in the city was safe, as long as she was breathing. She'd demonstrated to him her vicious capabilities when she murdered Sugar in cold blood! When she said, she would do him ten times worse if he didn't take the money and shut the fuck up, he felt he didn't have a choice. He just took the money and really didn't think too much of it until Joey was found dead in the football player's house.

He had no doubt that it was her! There was nowhere he could go without taking that extra glance over his shoulder. He only went to nightclubs, where he knew the owner or bouncers would let him in with his piece. In case, the crazy bitch tried to run him down; he would be ready. The figure he saw, while gazing over his shot glass, took his mind on a short vacation. He nearly swallowed his ice at the sight of her tanned red skin and her hazel eyes. Her build was unlike any ordinary, white chick. Her curves bulged from her clothes. She sat next to Juju, and their conversation started immediately. There were a few white girls in the club, but if there was one he could take to his room, it would definitely be her! Their conversation lingered on for hours. He stayed, longer than expected. She was just what he needed, a stress reliever. There was no way he was leaving without her pretty, white ass tonight.

"Let's go find somewhere… more comfortable to talk," he said, smiling, and showing his gold teeth. "Someplace like where?" she asked, really sassy.

"I tell you what," she continued, "If you're still here, with two of the shots by the time I return, I may give it some consideration," she said, leaving her seat and going to the restroom.

The way she looked from the front was an illusion, and it was her backside that complemented her shape.

"Good God!" Juju uttered, staring at her ass bounce from side to side, rubbing his hands together as she walked away.

"Bartender, give me two more doubles!" he yelled. The Bartender gave him a look of concern, as he poured their drinks.

"What the fuck you looking at, nigga?" Snapped Juju, feeling the full effects of the shots he had earlier.

Without saying a word, the old man shook his head, gave Juju his drinks, and walked away.

He couldn't believe he, "was about to fuck this sexy muthafucka," he thought as he watched her make her way back through the crowd to sit with him.

"This must be my lucky night," he thought, motioning for her to take a seat, before handing her the drink.

"I see you haven't left," she said, smiling, covering the top of her glass with her hand exposing the white substance to the liquor.

"Why would I leave when you are, leaving with me?" Juju asked, still mesmerized by this opportunity.

"You are mighty sure of yourself, aren't you?" she said, twirling the glass in her hand so the powder could mix in good with the drink, giving him a seductive smile.

"You're either confident or losing, is what I was told," said Juju, checking his surroundings for Tammy or her hitmen.

"Yes, you right, confidence is key," she responded, switching out their glasses the moment Juju's head was turned.

"You damn right!" said Juju, grabbing the shot off the table, downing it like it was the last of the liquor left in the club.

"Oh, baby! My pager is going off, let me check this," she said, excusing herself from the bar and making a quick exit for the door.

"Where in the fuck! That bitch going?" thought Juju, as he up stood from his seat, trying to scan the club for her. He noticed the dance floor looking kind of blurry, and his legs felt like rubber bands once his feet hit the floor. The crowd watched as a few girls screamed, watching his body fall to the floor, shaking fiercely. Foam erupted from his mouth with his eyes rolling to the back of his head, as he gave off a rattle, similar to a snake. A crowd gathered around him in a circle, and the music stopped as they watched. One guy rushed to Juju's aid and administered CPR, trying to save him.

"Someone, call 911!" he yelled, "I think he's dying!"

After ditching her wig in the dumpster and removing the contacts from her eyes, she changed her outfit, then met Roper at a small diner on the outskirts of the city, to recover her retainer. The diner was relatively empty: a perfect place for the drop. When she arrived, Roper was sitting at the far back table in the corner of the diner, ashing a cigarette.

She could tell he was anxious by the way he played with the butt of his cigarette; thumping ashes that weren't there. Figuring she would save him the anguish once she sat down, she jumped straight to it.

In a quiet, unforgiving tone, she said, "It's done."

"That's great! Did you make sure lots of people were around?" Roper asked. He felt it was imperative a lot of witnesses saw him die from nothing more than a stroke. People believed what they 'saw and most of the time, what they 'heard.' So why not give them something out of a "Hollywood playbook" to clear Tammy's name. He stayed up for nights, making sure his plan was brilliantly executed. He didn't bother including Tammy, after the comment she made, about putting Cory on ice. He thought that maybe she was getting ahead of herself, and it was time to create distance between them before she got out of hand.

The white girl came highly recommended by an outside source. She'd followed Juju around for days, making sure the timing and volume of people were perfect. Feeling a little offended, from Roper questioning her expertise, she mocked him, "Dose the club have enough people for you?"

"Yes that's perfect," Roper said, retrieving the manila envelope from his jacket pocket and sliding it underneath the table to her.

Glimpsing under the table, she scrolled through the stuffed bills with her thumb before putting the money in her pocketbook.

"It was nice doing business with you... Sir," she said, winking her eye.

He simply just nodded his head in agreeance, as they parted ways.

CHAPTER 12
Last Laugh

*I*t had been months since Tammy or the Mayor heard from Roper, and they were both starting to feel the impact of his absence. Tammy was down to her last few bricks she'd stored for herself. She told her crew to put a heavy cut on each brick. This allowed her to save a brick here and there, but now she was cutting into her stash. After she gave Roper the last payment, he went off the grid. Out of desperation, she played the last card she had and reached out to Mayor Ford. Although they'd never met, she felt that the least he could do is give her Roper's location. She soon came to find out her request wouldn't be as easy as she'd thought.

Tammy entered the elevator. She was nervous about meeting the Mayor for the first time. She didn't know what to expect. If he was anything like the stories she'd had heard, she hoped at the bare minimum her attire would have him see things her way. She fixed her skin-tight dress as she stepped in the elevator. She felt the guy in the suit next to her, undress her with his eyes. She peered at him coldly then gave off a smirk when she noticed him quickly, focus on the elevator door as it opened.

After getting off the elevator, she felt a little more confident. She thought to herself, 'the dress she had on just may get her the answers she needed.' Adjusting her outfit once more, she knocked on the Mayor's office door.

"Come in!" he said, in a raspy country, slurry voice. As she entered his office, she was surprised to see the huge Confederate flag framed to the wall behind his desk. She took note of the pictures and statues of Robert E. Lee and all the Confederate soldiers that decorated his office.

She thought, "Damn! Do black people even vote?" She kept a smile on her face as she shook his hand.

Returning the smile and displaying his pearly white dentures, he gestured with his hand for her to take a seat.

"Well, let me start off by saying, it's my absolute pleasure to finally have a chance to meet you in person, Ms. Jackson, from Akins. I believe you had an uncle by the name of Cowboy... am I correct?" said Ford, throwing around his authority, revealing his card too soon.

Trying her best to maintain a smile, she managed to force out, "Yes, you're correct, Mr. Mayor." Coming to grips they weren't playing on a leveled playing field, she continued, "but do me a favor and just call me Tammy, ok?"

"Hmm," the Mayor motioned while nodding in agreement. "Now, Cowboy... he was murdered. He and that precious little girl! That was such a tragedy," said the Mayor, shaking his head but trying to appear as sincere as possible. The Mayor wanted the day to himself to fight off the hang over that drowned his brain and was frustrated she was there in the first place. He had canceled all his meetings and was surprised she slipped through the cracks.

"Hey! I bet you didn't know my campaign was built around that tragic incident. After that terrible, terrible incident, I valued to make Columbia's streets safer and damn it! That's exactly what I'm going to do!"

"Lord, help us," Tammy mumbled. The thought of this racist, psychopath leading their city, sickened her.

"Yeah, that sounds great, Mayor," she said full of sarcasm, seeing directly through his bullshit.

"So, let me ask you this, Sweetie-do you really believe, out of all the people in this great state, that it takes City Hall to pedal drugs throughout the community?"

'This black bitch is playing politics with me,' he thought, feeling his pecker, slightly jump from the strong, radiant attitude she displayed from across his desk.

"It's about control, sweetheart," he continued. "If I control the traffic, then I control the violence. The simple fact is, animals need to be tamed, caged and controlled," he said while relieving himself from his seat and looking into her blistering brown eyes. Noticing Tammy's frustration only turned him on even more. He'd seen the look a million times before and they all broke to his will. He thought, 'she would be no different.'

"What you people don't understand is the big picture. Just like Curtis's death was necessary for you, Cowboy's death was a necessity for me," he said, shoving his thumb in his chest while locking his office door.

Tammy immediately lunged from her seat. "What the hell is going on, Mayor!?"

"Sit down, Tammy, I'm only locking the door because of my staff! We don't need them interrupting our conversation, now, do we?" he said, giving off his best drunken lover boy impression.

The look in his eyes let her know what the sleazy, drunk bastard, was up to. She thought to herself, 'the dress is doing a better job than I anticipated,' giving herself an inside smile.

"No, we don't," she replied, giving him direct eye contact, almost teasing his flirtatious ways. Her eyes turned bedroom, and all the hate that resided in them seemed to fade away.

Pulling his chair from underneath his desk, he said, "So enlighten me... why do I have the pleasure of meeting your acquaintance, Tammy?" The Major reached for his stash and poured himself a double shot of bourbon, before offering her any.

She quickly waved off his offering, and he nonchalantly shrugged his shoulders. He took a chug straight out the bottle, then threw it back into the bottom drawer of his desk while she continued saying, "To be honest, I need to find Roper, Mr. Mayor. Do you think you can help me?"

Studying the mild crack of desperation coming from her voice, he dove in for the kill! Like an eagle, with his claws extended.

"Well, the way things get done in my world, the political one is one hand washes another, sweetheart," he responded.

"That's the only way things get accomplished around here girly," the Mayor said smiling lewdly, through his devilish eyes, peering at her while finishing his brown temptation in a glass in one sip.

"And, what's your price, baby?" she asked, watching him grope himself in ways a thirsty trick would after the money has been exchanged.

"The price is you, lil lady," answered the Mayor while walking slowly towards her and quickly jumping into role play, giving his best John Wayne impression.

Her thick brown thighs teased him through her skin-tight dress. Thinking he wasn't living anything short of his best life, his belt buckle hit the ground as he whipped out his wrinkled pecker, in front of her face.

"Wouldn't you love to have some of this pretty, wet, pink pussy?" she said in a tone, sweet and softer than the smoothest jazz, you would ever want to hear. Sliding her fingers through the creased spilled of her dress, anticipating his lack of self-control, she added a wink.

His head bobbed up and down like a doll, and his tongue hung like a K9's! As he uncontrollably panted from excitement, he yelled. "Beat me, beat me!" Dropping to the floor on all fours, putting his pale white-ass up for display, while pointing at the closet door on the far side of his office for the hidden whips and chains of his silent life.

She wanted to bust out in laughter, seeing the Mayor on his hands and knees begging! So much power hidden, smothered by the temptations of his desires. It took everything out of her, not to get a whip from the closet and give him a good crack across his back! Instead, she shoved one of his ass cheeks with her foot, kicking him to the floor.

"Get up, nigga!" She said, exposing the recording device she had stuffed in her pocketbook, pressing stop.

The drunk he had, quickly faded away, with his semi-boner. He stared at the small tape recorder in her hand, as she unveiled an evil smile; exposing her true intentions.

Holding out both of his hands in shame, but still, on his knees, he pleaded, "Honey! You really don't want to do this- Do, ya?"

"So, is that the favor you gave to sustain your power?" she said with a smirk, referring to him on his knees.

Quickly jumping to his feet, fixing his clothes, he protested, "Now, now young lady you listen up!"

"No, no,-You listen up!!"

A click came from the tape recorder in her hand. His voice was loud and clear, exposing murder and sexual misconduct. She held a life sentence in her hand with his own voice as a key witness.

"You know, blackmailing a public servant is against the law, don't you, Young lady?!"

"Of course, I do, sweetheart," she said, flashing another devilish smile as she continued. "But this tape proves you are a servant of self and if anything happens to me," she threatened, {setting the recorder back in her purse}. "Or if you decide to play stupid, I will make sure your abused, lily, white ass is plastered over every news station in America. You got that, pervert?!!" Her face gave no signs of jokes, and the Mayor wasn't taking it for one.

His back was against the wall; he was stuck! He put a number of people in these same shoes, and it was time for him to wear a pair that he wasn't willing to pay for. But he slipped his toe in, mid sneaker, and while taking a seat, he said, "What is it that you want? Roper? His money? Hell, I haven't heard from him in weeks; in almost a full mouth! Ever since he decided to adopt that nig... black boy! You know? The one whose family was killed!"

"You mean, James?"

"Yes, that one!" he said, without one ounce of remorse.

It was that very moment she realized that the Devil played on all platforms! Both high and low-even though she was the one who put him there. After seeing James mourn in the hospital over his family {the same way she once did}and witnessing the Government offices that were supposed to give a fuck, not caring, made her accept it was a low country; a city of snakes. She knew there weren't a reptile's teeth that dug deeper or had deadlier venom than hers. Her mind was made up! She was going to take the racist son of a bitch's career to its grave if it was the last thing she did! Her personal mission just became "intimate."

"You know all I wanted was your flunkey's address! But now, I want the whole dam operation!! If you don't want this tape getting into the wrong hands, you will do everything I say from here on out! You got that?"

"You black bitch! Did you think I would let your nappy head ass con me? Ha!" The Mayor busted out loudly.

"How do you think I got here? I am the con, bitch! And by the way; who do you think made your uncle and that precious little girl such a great sound bite?!!

Heated rage moved from her stomach to the top of her head. She wanted to snatch the 22' from her purse and put his brains on the Confederate flag behind him. 'Why set herself up for the death penalty?' She thought, besides, by the time she was done with him, he would want to kill himself, anyway! The thought calmed her down as she reached in her pocketbook for the tape recorder, instead of her strap. Getting up from her seat with a blissful calmness and waving the recorder in the air, she said, "Well, we will do things your way then, Mr. Mayor." She smiled, as she headed towards the door. She knew he wouldn't just give his career up so easily, so she wasn't surprised when he called for her, no sooner than her hand touched the doorknob.

She said nonchalantly, "what is it, Man?" staring at the huge wooden door in front of her.

"What do you want? Money? That's all you people ever want! Well, I have plenty of it!" he yelled, watching her walk out of his office, with his future, slamming the door behind her.

"Fucking black bitch!" he mumbled while picking up the heavy office phone and taking a deep sigh.

After a few rings, the Chief of police answered the phone.

"Hello, Chief! How are you, old buddy?"

"I'm just fine, Mr. Mayor, thanks for asking."

"That's great, and how about Barbra and the kids?"

"Yea, yea, yea! Everyone is fine but cut the bullshit! I'm a busy man, Mr. Mayor. Now, how can I be of help?"

"I have a big, black, thorn in my ass, Chief!"

The Chief chuckled, "Well I hope you're not expecting me to pull it out for you!"

"I don't have the patience or the time, to entertain your buffoonery. Now, I got this black, hell spawn bitch, threatening to ruin me. So if my ass is on the line, so is yours! I'm sure you're familiar with the protocol, aren't you?" said the Mayor, pausing for a second with his dry threats. He walked in circles around his office while holding the base of the wired phone in one hand.

He continued, "So, I am sure we have a clear un-derstanding, if them backstabbing, Yankee sons of bitches in Washington open my file, then rest assured, as a dog licks his own damn balls, they will open them all! And we have a certain colleague whose name we don't ever want to resurface. Do we understand each other here, Chief?"

"Yes, Sir! What's her name?"

"Tammy, Tammy Jackson; can you believe that she's the niece of my old informant?"

"Who, Cowboy?"

"Yeah son, that bastard! I want you to label her black ass armed and dangerous! Kill on sight, if you have to, but let me warn you, son, that bitch is slicker than a bowling lane with baby oil. So just make sure you don't get yourself in a mess like you did last time."

"Oh! Don't you worry, Mr. Mayor! I'll put my best guys on it! Is there anything else I can do for you this evening, Sir?"

"Yes, as a matter of fact, there is. Later I want you to stop by my office to discuss the small details."

The Chief agreed, before hanging up. He was just as trapped, like everyone else in City Hall and the Mayor would only ruin him. There were a lot of things the Mayor did that he didn't agree with. For example, Cowboy; he thought it could have been handled with a lot more care. It was sloppy, but they made it work in the end.

CHAPTER 13
City of Snakes

arlier in time, when the Mayor was just Chief, he'd formed a group of seven he called, the "Lone Rangers." They started off robbing black gamblers, busting up dice and card joints then eventually became rogue. They murdered and sometimes raped their own kind. He knew what they were doing was wrong. He was young, wild, rich, and the police. The Chief now was the only deputy and wanted nothing more than to become a Lone Ranger. So, he joined them, fresh out of recruitment training. He didn't have to go through shit like some of the other guys. His dad and Ford were friends since they were kids.

He was raised in the Klan, and his family would rave about how the Rangers were local heroes for the white cause. As a teenager, they became his idols, and there wasn't anything more he wanted to be but a Ranger. That's until he actually joined the group of thugs in uniform and realized, they were nothing more than some murdering thieves that cared about nothing but themselves. By the time he figured that out, he was nothing more than the Chief's puppet. Ford had already generated a report on him that would put him away for life. It wasn't only him, the Chief had documented reports on. Crimes, places, names of politicians, lawyers, judges, you name it; Ford was blackmailing everyone, He kept the information safely hidden, and he never missed an opportunity to let them know. He had the dirt that could turn their lives upside down. Everything changed that night they all met at the bowling alley. It was one of those places where there were more blues than civilians. They were highly favored by most of the Department. The deputies that really didn't care for them wouldn't dare say it. The Chief had the strong arms of the law choke-holding everyone outside of the Rangers. The precinct's jobs were on a tight rope, and they walked as if they knew it.

When all seven of them assembled around a table in the corner of the bowling alley, most knew just to leave them alone. For the deputies that didn't know any better, they would insult them so badly it would make them do one of these three things. Fight, resulting in immediate suspension. Stand around and listen to them railroad your wife and kids so harshly you would want to quit the whole damn job; or do what most did and simply ignore them altogether.

Surrounded by his legion of goons, Chief Ford sat at the head of the table with deputy Roper Sr. as his right-hand man. The meeting was mandatory, although everyone pretty much had a clue of what it was about. Crack cocaine was starting to sweep through Columbia like wildfire, and it was time for them to get in on the action! The original plan was to move it through the black neighborhoods by some of the loyal snitches they had on the take. The Chief deceived them into thinking this would be the best thing for the city. If they controlled the drugs; they controlled the crime. If they controlled the crime; they controlled the neighborhoods. At the time, it seemed like a great idea, and everyone was on board. That is, until the floodgates started to slowly open, exposing the trailer park to the filth they fed the city, and eventually, the plague found its way into some of their homes.

In the beginning, John Roper Sr. tried to ignore it, but his wife's addiction was eating her alive, like a vulture's peck ripping pieces of dead flesh from a deprived corpse. She was starting to lose weight in her face, and not even makeup could hide the bruises left by crack. People around town were starting to whisper. While Roper Sr. was on the beat, his wife was on the street doing whatever it took to taste the rock at the end of her glass dick.

Once word got around the department his wife was spotted on the darker side of the tracks giving a blow job to some nigger in an ally, it shattered his pride! The laughter behind his back, with the insinuation of him not being man enough, was at its worst, especially since he was second in command of the Rangers.

"He's too weak to handle his own wife," they would say, walking by, just loud enough for him to hear.

"A nigger's dick, can you believe it?" Some even made sure he heard them, by looking over their shoulder, while cracking a goofy grin.

That was the straw that broke the camel's back. He checked himself in a rehab center with hopes of his wife doing the same. He knew that for her, it wouldn't be an easy road. He'd seen junkies come in and out of the system and the withdrawals sometimes could be deadly. It seemed like locating her would be harder than checking her into rehab. One night, he drove around for hours until dawn broke; checking every ally and crack house he could think of. He felt it was all his fault! His wife would be home with his son if he hadn't exposed the city to the Chief's greed. All he wanted now, was for her to return home safely with the hope of getting her into rehab.

The next day at the office was like any other day. The snickering and the cowardly jokes seemed to simmer down. Sitting at his desk while finishing paperwork, he noticed a shadow blocking the direct sunlight, shining on his desk.

"Ay Roper, when you stuck your pecker in your wife last night, did her cunt hole feel different?" said the young deputy loudly so everyone in the room could hear.

The room erupted with laughter as the young officer gloated in their applause. Without giving it a second thought, Roper lunged from his seat, snatching the young deputy by the collar! If he wasn't one of the seven, he would have killed him on the spot! His mind screamed 'murder,' as he reached for his sidearm.

"Calm down old buddy, I'm just teasing ya, Ranger!" said the young deputy, patting him on the shoulder.

"You really need to get that chip off your shoulder, Son. Hell, we all brothers in here, right?" He said loudly so the whole office could see the situation had been defused.

The brotherly cheers weren't as loud as the insult laughter, as a matter of fact, there weren't any cheers at all.

"The Boss wants ya, boy," murmured the young deputy, leaning in his ear, as he patted him on the shoulder and began leading the way.

"Here he is, Chief!" the young man said, giving Roper the courtesy of walking through the door first, then closing it behind them.

The Chief's office had a stench of cigars and scotch when they entered. He had the windows open with the intention of airing out his office of smoke, and it worked, but the odor from the cigar was so strong, it seemed to bleed in his fabric.

"Have a seat, Roper," said the Chief, lighting up another cigar. He watched Roper leaned back in his chair, and continued, "It was brought to my attention that you are having problems at home, with the wife. Maybe that's the reason your performance here is so piss poor, Son! What I am going to suggest is that you take a few weeks off. Then, you can straighten out your wife and son, then come back to work with a fresh sound mind. How does that sound? That sounds great, right?!" Said the Chief smiling, giving Roper a hand-shake.

Reluctantly, Roper agreed, "That sounds great Chief, I could use the time off. Besides, a few weeks out of this place might do me some good."

"I knew that it would, there's just one more thing I have to tell, ya," said the Chief, looking in the corner of the room at the deputy. "The rookie will be second in command of the Rangers."

"What!"

What he just heard crushed him. He had risked his life for the department but he put his soul on the line for the Rangers, some of the guys he still considered his brothers. Hell, he helped form the Rangers; how could he be thrown out of something he gave life to?? "And just what in the hell, do you mean that the fucking rookie is second in command?!" Roper barked, snaring at the rookie who held a silly smirk, that he unsuccessfully tried to hide.

"I put it all on the line for the Rangers! My life, my precious wife…"

"Speaking of your wife," replied the rookie, "where was she last night? Because last I heard, she was in Niggerville sucking some monkey's dick!" he chuckled.

Roper gripped firmly to his sidearm, slightly brandishing it from the holster.

"Now, now… see that's exactly the kind of behavior we can do without at this precinct. Hand me your badge and your sidearm, deputy!" the Chief said, reaching for Roper's sidearm.

"Don't make me do this, Son!" he said, noticing the rookie had a real itchy finger.

Roper peered around the room. He was outgunned, but he made sure Ford knew he wouldn't go out without a fight.

"Fuck you, Ford!" he stated quietly.

"Fuck you!" he barked, "I gave my life to this hell hole! You won't get away with this; I am going to bury you, you fucking snake!"

"Clean out your desk and get the hell out of my precinct!" yelled the Chief. The Chief's eyes were pitch black as if there was no sign of life in them as he said, "Boy, the next time you threaten me, it will be your last breath."

After weeks of apologizing and begging, Roper convinced Ford to let him get back on the force. He assigned him to traffic duty. It was the most hated job in the precinct, but he didn't mind. He was a cop again, and that's all that mattered. His wife was on her tenth week at an inpatient rehabilitation center and was doing better. She was starting to look like the Barbie she once was. She was even coming home sooner than he thought. Although a lot of the guys at the station joked about his wife, here and there, he didn't let it bother him anymore. He felt free. Free from the chains and snares of the Chief. For the first time in a long time, he started looking forward to the future. As soon as he saved enough money, he would leave this; the city he was convinced, God had forgotten about.

Today was a special day for Roper and his family. His wife was getting out of rehab after twelve weeks. He was excited, not only for her but for his son as well. It seemed, the closer the time came for her to come home, the more his son asked about her. He would tell him, "Don't you worry, ya mind none, son... Ya, mother is just away on business, she'll return home soon."

He was only 15, but he knew that was a lie. His mom never had a job until she started leaving at night. Sometimes she would be gone days at a time. And there were rumors around the school from kids who overheard their parents gossiping. They called his mamma a crack whore and a nigger lover. In the beginning, the rumors bothered him so suspension and detention became a common routine. And, just like his dad, the gossip became numb to him over time.

John Roper could hardly sleep the night before picking up his wife from the rehab center. He'd dropped young Roper off at his grandparents the night prior. He didn't want him seeing his mother leaving some hospital like a mental patient. Plus, he had guidelines and rules he wanted to explain to her before they arrived home. For example, she was no longer able to handle any more cash without his presence. That was a sure way to stir up an argument, as well as some of the other rules he had in place. He figured he would jump those hurdles, once it showed its face.

The morning air was brisk but warm. Most people had already gone to work, and his surroundings were quiet. That is, except for the chirping from the birds giving off a façade of peace in the air. Roper positioned himself comfortably in his seat before placing the key in the ignition. He put the car in gear, reached over his seat to check his rear, when a Ruger stuffed in his temple met him! The car was so quiet Roper could hear his own heartbeat. The gunman watched as Roper slowly reached for his firearm.

"Do me a favor and hand me that sidearm, Roper!" the gunman said, pressing the pistol snugged to his temple, causing his head to move.

"Here you go, you son of a bitch!" said Roper, as he threw the gun to the backseat.

"Why? Why are you doing this?" he pleaded.

Ignoring Roper, the gunman said, "Leave your neighborhood, make a right, and go straight, till I tell you to stop."

Recognizing the disguised voice in the backseat, Roper turned around and blurted out, "Rookie?!"

"You never did know how to keep your fucking mouth shut, now did you, Roper?"

"The Chief knows you're doing this? When we get to the station Imma make sure your ass is burning with the cross."

"You fucking... idiot! Who do you think ordered it?" the rookie said, bursting out with laughter.

"You know, Roper, I always liked you," he said, "but I always found your wife's sweet ass to be more entertaining! That woman can blow a cucumber through a straw. Have you ever fucked her while she was on that shit? I tell you, Roper, you definitely have yourself a wild one," he said while reaching in his pocket for a can of snuff while glaring over his shoulder to see if they were still being trailed.

"You know, Roper?" said the gunman, leaning over the seat and pointing the gun in his direction, "She was so good, in fact, once I was done with the crack whore, I sold her to the Chief! Can you believe that greedy bastard kept her for himself?? He promised that bitch the world, telling her he would take care of her and your son, once she got out of rehab. That is where you were going, right?"

Roper felt like he'd been baptized in the lake of fire! The guys he'd once called brothers had come to kill him after they've been feeding his wife drugs and forcing her to turn tricks! He slammed on the brakes as hard as he could, forcing the Rookie out the backseat, crashing his head on the dashboard and knocking him unconscious.

"What a fucking, ass hole!" he said, recovering his gun from the backseat along with the weapon the Rookie dropped on the floor from the dashboard impact. Roper quickly jogged to the passenger side of the car. He grabbed the Rookie from the passenger floorboard and dragged him to the highest patch of grass he could find. He checked his surroundings and noticed a truck that was so far down the road, they couldn't have witnessed anything credible. He raced back to his car. The sound of an engine, barbarically ribbing, was closing space towards him fast. His heart raced, expecting the loud truck to be one of the Chief's traps.

The truck zoomed right by him! He took a breath; calming himself down, as he searched for his car keys. He cracked a smile at the sight of the Rookie's chewing tobacco, mixed with blood splattered on his dash. After putting his key in the ignition, Roper heard an engine similar to the one that had just passed him. Except for this time, they abruptly stopped. Rubber smoke burned from the back tires as the full-size truck blocked him in. Two masked men who were dressed in black, leaped from the truck, brandishing automatic weapons. A hail of bullets hit Roper's windshield all at once, killing him instantly. One of the masked men helped the Rookie, buried in the grass, while the other doused gasoline over Roper's car. Then, they loaded up, drove by the bullet-riddled car and flicked a match, igniting a fire.

After the department gave their bogus narrative to the news a few days later, two black guys were arrested and charged with the "murder" of an officer. They apparently recovered a murder weapon, fingerprints, and had a witness — just enough fraudulent evidence to send two innocent ex-cons to the chair. News of police corruption soon became a headline story, and the Rangers began disassociating themselves, to save face. The Chief was never questioned, just most of the deputies and as fast as the allegations of corruption appeared, they disappeared.

CHAPTER 14
Exposed

After leaving City Hall, Tammy knew exactly what she needed to do. The Mayor was a cancer to the city, and he needed to be surgically removed. He destroyed her life and then boasted about it to her face! She wished she could make him choke on his dentures and die. He was an outright evil person, and the world could do without him. He was too powerful for her ever to get that close again, so she would destroy his reputation, his career, and everything he ever worked for. She wanted to see him burn!

Turning in the parking lot of the Daily Journal, she thought, "This is it, she and her son's life would never be the same, once she exposed the Mayor's wicked ways." Wanting to remain anonymous, she slid the tape recorder in a manila envelope that read, "Important!!! Please, give to a trusted journalist."

The Daily Journal was busy with a lot of moving parts. It was hard to decipher between a journalist and a civilian with the naked eye. She was playing with father time, so she had to trust her gut instinct. She scanned through the lobby to find a trusting face. She locked eyes with the security guard who stood by the elevator with his hands in his pocket, examining the faces coming and going. He wore a friendly old wrinkled smile on his dark-skinned face. She rushed towards him, cutting through the crowd while holding the envelope by her side, as she read his morality. He wore his seniority on his jacket, furthermore, letting her know he'd been working for the company awhile. Her gut also told her, he was perfect. She slipped the package between his hip and partial palm draping from his pocket and leaned in his ear, saying, "I'm trusting you will give this to the right person?" Never waiting for an answer, she faded in the crowd.

Time was not on her side. She still had to get to the cash she'd stashed in the condo and drive to the country to pick her son up. If she was lucky, she could bless one of her cousins with a great deal on a few kilos. She hated leaving her son with her abusive mother, but her life was "murder," and the less the streets knew, the better she felt. After meeting Big, her mission was clear. Being a full-time parent wasn't going to get it done, so she gave full custody to her mother, maiden name, and all.

The hundreds of dollars she sent every month would be more than enough to carry them over. Her son lived project rich, while she enjoyed the finer things in life, she could never own, until now. It was time for her to introduce him to what she never saw growing up; prosperity. She had it all planned out. She would move to Alabama and buy land for a low price to build her dream home on. The time had finally come. She was feeling Roper's direction of change. Besides, how much money could she make? The $400,000 she'd saved was more than enough playing this game. Once she sold the few keys she had and picked up her son, it would be the beginning to her brand-new life.

After months of rehab, James was back on his feet. The senseless death of his family haunted his dreams at night and sometimes merged with the days. Out the corner of his eye, he often could see and feel his mother's presence. After being released from the hospital, Coach surprised James with a house in the city of Casey and a sports car. He laid in a single size hospital bed for months, not knowing where he would go the day they released him. The pressure had gotten to him, stress hidden behind a smile of courage. There were plenty of nights he laid helpless and alone with tears pouring from his cloudy eyes and reminiscing about his mother.

He couldn't see a way out. He thought his world had ended; his football career was trashed, along with his life. He had no idea why he had trouble remembering day-to-day events and couldn't recap a clip of what happened the night of the slaughter. The doctors told him he would have problems recalling events for a while, but the day Coach handed him the keys to his own house and car, was a day he wouldn't soon forget. Roper even stayed with him until he was strong enough to move around by himself.

He knew Roper couldn't afford the car, house, and the crazy amounts of cash that he just threw in his lap, on a coach's salary! Nevertheless, he never asked questions. He would simply thank him, and every time, Roper would respond jokingly, "Don't worry son, you will pay me back every clean penny." At first, it bothered James. Coach knew damn well he didn't have that type of money to repay him. But what he didn't' know, is that Coach had a plan and in time, he would find those ideas to be false.

Eggs and Bacon sizzled, giving the kitchen a southern morning smell. He had Wu Tang Klan, "Cream" ringing through the entire house. He flipped eggs and bobbed his head to the tune of the beat as he rapped along, "Cash rules everything around me, Cream get the money. Got a dollar bill y'all."

A faint ring from the doorbell nearly went unheard. The music was so loud in the mid-size house. James turned down the high flames under his breakfast and answered, "Who is it?" as he yelled over the loud music.

"It's Mo! Grace's father!" he answered back.

"Oh, shit!"

"Hold on a second!" he said, turning down the music and hiding the roaches in the ashtray, under the couch.

"Here I come!" he yelled, spraying a trail of air fresher through the house, creating a path to the door.

"Boy, it's damn good to see you back on ya feet!" said Mo, cracking the grays on his cheek, smiling and holding out his arms to give a bear hug to the injured superstar.

"A lot of people didn't think you would make it, boy. But, then again, that's what's wrong with people. They think too damn much," he said with a chuckle, patting James on the shoulder.

As he walked in the mid-size house, he said, "Boy, people around the Diner been telling me how Roper got you in a nice, fly pad. Hell, I had to come and see for myself."

"Yeah, Coach really outdid himself with this one," said James, walking up the stairs, leading Mo to the living room.

"Son, I know you don't want to hear this," Mo said, taking a seat on the couch, dialing down his tone to serious. He knew Roper was a snake. He watched him turn his nephew into a monster, and he would be damned if he sat back and watched him do the same to James. He continued, "Son, just because a man shines like an angel in your time of need doesn't mean he's God. Roper is a wolf in sheep's clothing…"

James cut him short, "Not to be disrespectful, Mr. Mo… but Coach is the only person who did anything for me, and all you can do is call him a snake! That's some messed up stuff to say, Mr. Mo."

Mo, pounced to his feet, leveling eye contact with James, "Look here, Son! Roper is nothing but a damn drug dealer! Hell everyone knows it!! How in the hell do you think he can afford all this shit? My advice to you is, 'get out!' Get out while you have a chance, Son!"

James just stood paralyzed, dazed even, but he didn't doubt the authenticity of his accusations. "Drugs?" he thought, trying to soak it all in. He figured Roper probably inherited the bread or something. To him, most white people had money, anyway. Roper was on the solo list of the white people he knew outside the school. Besides, every white person he met had money, even some of the junkies in his old hood drove BMWs.

"Son," said Mo, "I know, this may be a hard pill to swallow. Hell, I had trouble believing it myself, but once I put it all together; it made perfect sense. My nephew Cory told me, Roper brought that sleazy tramp, Tammy to the hospital with him."

Noticing the confused look James displayed, Mo grabbed him by the shoulder and said, "Listen up, Son! That she-devil is dangerous." For a few seconds, Mo stared at the floor, like there was a hidden message on it he couldn't decode.

"I don't know how to tell you this, son, but word is… she killed Sugar because she knew Tammy robbed my nephew Big. I think that slithery bitch tried to kill you, too! I just can't figure out how Roper is involved," said Mo, stroking his stringy grays on his chin.

"So, are you telling me, Coach knows who killed my family, Mr. Mo?" James asked, tightening his eyebrows as he held in tears.

"All I know is that he knows a lot more than what he's putting on and the "book" will tell you that shit!"

Mo hated being the bearer of bad news and looking at James on the brink of breaking down, didn't make him feel any better. He hugged him and said, "Ay, I'll tell you what, James; why don't you come and stay with me, for a while? Grace is in school, so I have the room.

What do ya say, James? You can even work with Cory and me at the Diner, for money."

"Sure, Roper sold drugs," thought James, "but he wasn't the one that pulled the trigger." He owed Roper. No one ever looked out for him the way he has. He owed him his life, and although he respected Mo's opinion, he had heard enough. He had his own place and car, on the day he left the hospital. Roper had given him a better life, and he wasn't about to leave it to work with Mo at his Diner.

James was relieved when the doorbell rang. Although he was grateful for Mo's offer, his deal stunk. Besides, once he didn't want Grace coming around like his life was a burden on hers or some shit. The doorbell saved him from having to put him out or shut him up. Instead, he led him down the stairs towards the front door.

A voice came from outside the door. "It's Roper-open up, buddy!" he said, sounding more excited than usual. It didn't take long for Roper to grasp, why it took so long for James to answer the door, once he saw the hatred Mo wore in his eyes for him.

"I'll see you later, James," Mo said, giving Roper a stare that would kill if looks could. As he sucked his teeth, he bumped Roper's shoulder, on his way out.

"Damn, what the fuck is his problem!" said Roper, smiling off Mo's disrespect.

"You're a fucking drug dealer, Coach!" James shouted," That's his fucking problem! My fucking family's dead, that's the problem, Coach!"

He saw a look in Roper's eyes; one he'd never seen. He looked lost, somewhere in space, searching for the right words to ice his molded cake. He smelled his food burning in the kitchen. "All this shit is fucked up, Coach!" James continued. Jogging up the stairs, he could now smell the dull gray smoke from his food. The eggs and bacon had sizzled to a crisp! He thought he put the stove on the lowest temperature, but it turned out to be medium-high. Half of his memories were lost, and a lot of times he would have delusional "hiccups," like this one. Frustrated, he threw the pan on the floor! The burnt eggs splattered on the lower cabinet and the bacon, crumbled once it hit the ground.

Roper could partially relate to James's pain. He knew how tough it could be to bury a loved one under any circumstances. He stared at the mess on the floor and sighed, retrieving a smoke from his khaki shorts.

He said humbly, "Sit down and take a breather, Son. I'll take care of this." He lit his cigarette, then went to the closet for the dustpan and broom. He wished he could have been the one to expose his own façade, but the cat was out the bag. After he finished cleaning James's mess, he noticed he'd calm down. He figured it was time to lay it all on the table and just come clean.

Interrupting Roper's moral compass, James gave him a baffled glare and said, "Coach, I didn't know you smoked cigarettes!"

"Well son, it's a lot of things we have yet to know about each other. For example, I didn't know you smoke marijuana!" said Roper, reaching his hand underneath the sofa, finding the ashtray full of roaches.

"I spotted your stash coming up the stairs," Roper continued, with a grim smile and handing James the ashtray.

James carried the same look Roper had fifteen minutes prior. He snatched the ashtray from Roper's hand and said, "I was told this is the best thing for headaches!"

Roper chuckled, reaching in the ashtray James laid on the coffee table. He grabbed the mid-size blunt and straightened out the wrinkled end before firing it up.

James just sat there, with his mouth wide open, not believing his eyes. Once the blunt got around to him, he forgot he'd been pissed. They both stared at the wall in silence. Roper thought of how strong James had been to endure the amount of trauma he'd suffered.

After they had smoked the mid-size duby into a roach, Roper smothered its cherry in the ashtray. He peered at James with his glossy red eyes and said firmly, "when life gives you hurdles, don't jump over them; put your shoulder down and run through them. That way, when you're faced with the same hurdles again; you can walk over them. I know it's hard for you right now, son, but I can guarantee you this…together we will knock down those hurdles."

The pep talk didn't amuse James any. He felt it was time for Coach to be real with him. He wondered if the car and the house were meant to blind his truth. Could Coach have 'known his family would be slaughtered, like farm animals,' he thought, balling his face into a knot.

"So, Coach- them hurdles you were talking about? Let's knock one down now by you telling me who Tammy is?"

Roper swallowed a wad of spit as he frowned back into James's eyes. Everything in him wanted to flat out lie, but he thought, 'it might be too late for that.' He needed to 'find out what James knew and more importantly, he needed to find that bitch Tammy and ice her ass.' She knew entirely too much. He could kick himself a million times over for letting a pretty piece of ass and cocaine cloud his better judgment. Between the drugs and Tammy, his life was on a downward spiral.

After James was released from the hospital, he felt it was the perfect opportunity for them both to rehabilitate. He took some time away from the Mayor and Tammy. He laid off the cocaine for a while, and focused on their recovery, while getting intel on James's case from a couple of detectives that worked under the Chief. A month after moving out of James's house, he'd bought him, his nightmares and conscience ate at his skull. Curtis often hunted his dreams, cussing him viciously and his dreams usually ended in Curtis screaming, "I trusted you!" The more he stuck to his sobriety, the worse his nightmares became. Most nights, he would wake up in cold sweats, lack of sleep became common and he just wanted to forget his past. So he went back to his comforter drugs with the exception of him graduating from cocaine to "tracking" his arm.

The detectives told him there was a possibility that Curtis was never near the crime scene. A witness saw a masked person with a female physique, running through an alley before entering a vehicle. She'd played him like a bitch seeking advice from a mechanic. He helped murder his pupil for absolutely no reason at all. The thought of Curtis once saving his life, only for him to take his, made his stomach cringe. He thought of how he met her and the angle she played to kill Curtis. He wondered if she knew he pulled the trigger on the little girl in the photo and whether she could be coming for him next? Roper decided to give James the 'rundown on Tammy.' Besides, he deserved to know part of the truth. He told him he sold drugs until the day he left the hospital and had no idea Tammy was such a snake.

James' eyes were red and puffed, adding age to his young face. Sitting up with his elbows, he propped on his knees and glared at the king-sized TV as if he could see more than just a black screen. Roper figured, he knew exactly what James was going through. He had cried all the tears he could cry. His soul was like a desert; all dried up. Yep, Roper knew this feeling all too well. He also came up with a home remedy a few weeks prior, finding it hard to escape his pain. He found heroin to be a portal to freedom and thought that James was, maybe, in need of an early release. Reaching in his pocket, he pulled out a small bag of "boy."

With a grim smile and a low voice, he said, while dangling the sac of boy in James's face, "This is the shit that cures headaches, boy. Hell, the weed don't have shit on this. If weed's a vacation, this shit here is an escape," he said with enthusiasm, fetching a plate from the cabinet. He took a seat next to James and placed the small saucer on the coffee table. He poured half the bag on the miniature plate. He took a credit card from his wallet and cut into the tiny mountain of brown sugar, splitting it in half. Next, he rolled a tight C-note, offering it to James. It was an invitation for him to meet Mary Jane's fucked up side of her family.

James refused Roper's offer, waving his hands in the air and frantically shaking his head no. Roper simply shrugged his shoulder and sniffed the H in one nostril. Just as fast as the line disappeared from the saucer,

Roper was high. He slowly put the small plate on the table, as he laid snugged in the couch, smiling.

James didn't know how Roper felt, but whatever it was, it seemed to take his pain away. He looked at the eerie-blanked out a smile on his face and knew, where ever Roper was, that's where he was trying to go. Slowly he slid the C-note from between Roper's limped fingers and thought, "Man, he's fucked up, if I ran off with his hundred dollars, he wouldn't even notice." But, running off was the last thing he was going to do. James only knew his pain stabbed his heart, like a red-hot branded dagger. Once the dog food hit his brain, his skull exploded. He felt a tingling sensation, all over his body, especially his stomach. After his high wore down, and he came out his trans of delight, he discovered last night's chicken wings painted over his shirt. Roper assured him that it only happens the first time around and he was on his way to the twelve-step program of knocking hurdles down.

Ford's bottom denture could have fallen on his desk the next morning when he read the papers. The headline read, "Corruption in city hall," with his name plastered underneath it! As soon as he entered his office, his assistant purposely agitated the shit out of him. She knocked on his office door every time a reporter called fishing for the cover story. She hated the old bastard! She only kissed his ass for the check, and as far as she was concerned, the racist asshole probably deserved everything he was getting. She remembered the few times he aggressively came on to her and the constant disrespect she endured for marrying a black man. She wore a sinister smile that didn't show on her face. Today was her big, 'fuck you!' The shameful stress in his eyes when she entered his office, only made her giggle once she left.

Peeking through the metal blinds, Ford saw what looked like an army of reporters, on the front steps of City Hall. Protesters were starting to gather, and he knew the circus had come to town. When his assistant burst into his office again, he had had enough! This was her third time; her childish games caused him to over-react. Before she had a chance to utter a single word, without taking his eyes off the reporters outside, in a rough but settled country accent, he said without acknowledging her presence, "When I say, hold all calls that mean I don't want to be bothered!!" he fussed.

With his voice still settled, taking his focus from the reporters outside and directing it towards her, he continues, "Do us both a favor and leave for today. Go home to that nigger husband of yours and monkey fuck. You might get that right!" he said, turning his attention back to the reporters outside.

Her face bald with anger and her mouth dropped open, but not a word came out. She slammed the door, making the pictures rattle on the wall.

He snapped his head around when he heard the click from his office door opening. He had a good cussing out on tap if it was his annoying assistant. Instead of her, it was Roper peeking his pea head through the cracked door. He read the papers and seen the news. Things didn't look too good for the redneck. They had the cartoon version of him on his knees, tied up with a ball in his mouth, with bold letters that read, **"Whip me! Whip me!"**

For a prideful man like Ford, he knew the media's take on his news would crush him. So, he decided to drop in and visit him. It had been a while since he spoke to the Mayor, but due to his unfortunate circumstances, Roper thought he could use his council, or at the least, he could help him pack his things. What he heard after he came-in he didn't see coming, looking through bifocals in, a telescope.

Ford gave him a sweetened version of what took place with himself and Tammy. Then he blamed him for bringing the moonlighter around.

"Tammy!" he thought, 'that… bitch bites again.'

He considered the notion of this being Curtis's revenge. She put an ax in Ford's name and wisely murdered Curtis, with the naive help of yours truly. Lord only knows what she had planned for him, and he wasn't going to wait around contemplating the outcome. She had made a bed of nails, and he was the hammer, that would thrust her in it!

Interrupting Roper's thought process and giving the window a break, he rested his weary legs from his pointless stakeout and took a seat behind his desk.

"Where the hell have you been, Roper?" he said, with pure authority, dancing his loyalty around in his mind, then he quickly shunned the thought. He knew exactly where he was — somewhere getting high, playing godfather to that black boy. But, he didn't mind. With Curtis and Tammy out the picture and his career withering in the wind, the superstar, whose name he couldn't remember, might be the perfect addition to the family. Besides, with all the controversy surrounding him, Roper's trust was greatly needed. Soon, Washington would be on his tail about his buffoonery, and it wouldn't be easy for him to move around anymore. Roper, on the other hand, could move freely like a sovereign citizen.

Everything made sense; to hell with being the Mayor, he thought. He was going to run for Governor in a few years.

Ignoring the Mayor's question, Roper asked if he had Tammy's location. He knew the Mayor had the resources to find anyone regardless of where they were. She could hide, but it wouldn't be long before she was found. The Mayor's response was "no," but his guys were working around the clock until they could pinpoint her location.

Lighting a cigar, the Mayor said grimly, "She's a clever one. I think she's moving around under a different alias. But she will make a mistake, and when she does, my guys will be there."

Roper nearly felt sorry for the slippery moonlighter, he could only imagine what the old man would do to her. Once he got his greasy palms on her, her fate would be the same as Curtis's, he thought, shaking his head.

'Smart she is,' thought Roper, 'maybe a little too damn smart for her own good?'

"To be perfectly frank, Mr. Mayor, I don't think she's still in the state," Roper said humbly.

"I don't give a damn if the whore's in Timbuktu," the Mayor snapped back, "I will find her nigger ass and bring her here. Then ship her black ass back in pieces."

The thought of that gruesome scene sent chills up Roper's spine. By no means did he doubt the Mayor could pull it off. 'As for Tammy,' Roper thought, 'that poor girl is only running on fumes!'

CHAPTER 15
Tammy's Revenge

The new life that Tammy had built was nothing less than perfect. She convinced her cousin, with a few hundred dollars, to purchase a home in Alabama, using her name. This was a safety precaution she used to cover her tracks. Now she had a few acres of land, for her and her son, in a nice suburban area. She hid blocks of cash in the freezer and rubber-banded rolls of loot in cereal boxes. Needless to say, she had more than enough cash for such a slow lifestyle.

She would often go to church on Sundays and pray for God's forgiveness for her many deadly sins she committed in Columbia. In the mornings, she would sit on her enormous balcony and enjoy the cool autumn breeze. On nights, she read books under the stars and smoked herb. She had finally settled down to live the life she always dreamed of; the simple life, where she no longer had to sell drugs. Her son could play on the country land in peace, and her enemy's debts were paid. It didn't take long before her simple life became disastrous.

Two Sundays out of each month, she and her six-year-old son would put on their best for church. There she met a man of a few words. She was attracted to his smile and angelic personality. The bad boy roll had run its course, and she wanted to expose her son to a humbler type of man. She was convinced she'd hit the jackpot with her new boyfriend, Lue, who stood a few feet taller than she was and wore a complexion as dark as hers. He was great with her son. It made her smile to see them pitch the baseball back and forth, over the acres she owned. The look of freedom her son possessed, when he wore the slightly oversized glove, as he immensely concentrated for the ball, was priceless. More importantly, Lue the quiet, charismatic, young marine, made her happy. He was a breath of fresh air compared to the slum's smog, from which she came.

She thought life had finally taken its shackles of oppression and loveless bondage from her. She was just as free as her son playing catch in the backyard, and life couldn't be any better.

A few months into their relationship, things started taking a dark turn. After several attempts of asking to take Tammy out, Lue was ecstatic she'd finally agreed to let him take her on the town. He thought if he could loosen her up, with a few drinks, she would be prone to open dialogue. After three months, besides her name, where she lived, and the warm sweet juices of her womb, Lue knew very little about her, and she practically knew everything about him. She knew his friends and parents, where he went to school, everything down to his shoe size.

He really liked her and the kid, but the only time they were alone was during plumbing and pool boy hours. Then, when they were finished, relishing in satisfaction, he had to leave before the boy came home from school. She never allowed him to sleep over after dinners he shared with her and the kid. He sometimes stayed over a little later to watch a movie, but she made him leave after the matinee, of course. He felt like a piece of meat; a walking, talking dildo. He believed she was the perfect candidate for him to settle down with. He just didn't know anything about her. Her conversations were sweet but vague, and when he asked one too many questions, she would say, smiling with the sweetest country accent, "Boy, you sure are nosey," then switch the subjects like the question was never asked. 'Tonight would be different,' he thought. He wanted to make tonight more than their first, official date. He wanted them to officially become a couple.

Tammy was skeptical about leaving her son with Lue's parents. They were elders, and she feared they weren't able to keep up with him. He was a wild child and sometimes was a handful. They swore they would be ok and all they wanted in return was for Tammy and Lue to enjoy themselves and that's what they did! They drank liquor, sang karaoke, and danced. Time seemed endless and so did the cash, as she thoughtlessly bought shot after shot, constantly telling Lue not to worry about the tab. He was expecting to get her to open her heart, but instead, she opened her pocket book. She held so much money that it was bulging from her tiny hand. Curiously, Lue stared as she peeled a few C-notes from the top of her wad of cash.

"Tammy just be frank with me, baby," he said smoothly, lowering his voice with a heavy slur. "Who are you … what do you do for a living and how in the hell did you get all that money?" Lue said with a drunken step, catching his balance.

"I told you, once before sugar!" Tammy replied, just as wasted. Her mind took her to the D.A.'s sister she shot to death in Columbia, and she drunkenly blurted out again, "Sugar!" Exploding in tear dropping laughter.

Humiliated because he was being laughed at, like some circus clown in front of his peers, he started fussing. "What the fuck is so funny about getting to know the woman I've been fucking for the last three months?!" He shouted

The statement that he made, was heard around the whole bar. The entire room was silent so quiet that you could hear ashes from cigarettes fall in their trays. All eyes were on them as she reached for her mini purse on the table that concealed a couple of grand in loose hundreds, and a loaded 22' pistol.

"You know … I liked you much better when you were quiet," she said, propping a leg back as she leaned on her fist, crammed in her waist. She pointed her index finger, along with her pocketbook that she held tightly, towards his chest.

"Who would have thought? The big Marine is really a sensitive bitch!" she said belligerently in laughter as she lowered her purse to her waist side. The crowd engaged in the argument, and loud murmurs came from their audience.

"Well damn Lue, you going to let her talk to you like that?" said one of the onlookers in a deep heavy voice over the crowd. Lue looked towards the onlookers in shame as anger brewed in his heart. Besides the slight squinch in his eyes, no one could tell he was highly pissed.

He grabbed Tammy by the arm, "You're fucking embarrassing me!" he whispered aggressively. Feeling her resistance, as he forced her outside the bar.

She abruptly laughed, calling him weak and other derogatory names.

Lue opened the car door enraged and shoved her in. "Shut the fuck up, bitch! Shut the fuck up!" he snapped, slamming the passenger door.

"No, nigga, you shut the fuck up!" she said boldly as she slouched in the seat, no longer feeling the burn in her stomach, but just the dizzy after- effects of several double shots.

Watching drunkenly as Lue crank the car, she said, "You know what, nigga- just take me to get my child!" The evil glare Lue gave her went ignored. She simply rolled her eyes and taunted him to the 3rd degree. She cussed Lue loudly as he tried his best to focus on the road. The double shots he consumed were now giving him a head rush. The art of multitasking became difficult as they intensely fussed the car swerved from lane to lane. Once Lue realized his impairment reflected his driving, he tried concentrating on the road. His vision blurred as he leaned closer to the stirring wheel to regain focus. Flashing lights in his rearview mirror quickly sobered him up. Slowly pulling over, he angrily whispered, "Fuck!" Slapping his hand across the stirring wheel.

"Can I have your license and registration please?", the skinny, pale-faced officer said. Lue cracked a smile and gave the officer his military ID and registration, attempting to disguise his impairment.

"Are there any drugs or weapons in the car, sir?" the officer asked, directing the high beamed flashlight in Tammy's face.

"No, sir," Lue responded.

"Sir, have you been drinking?" he said, now flashing the light in Lue's eyes.

Trying to block the flashlight's rays with his hand and lying, Lue said, "Absolutely not, officer."

The cop suspiciously glared at Lue. Then directed his attention towards Tammy, "Do you have any ID, ma'am?"

To avoid an altercation, Tammy slightly opened her tiny purse, being careful not to reveal her loaded pistol and bankroll.

"Here you go, officer," she smiled, handing him her identification. After clearing their names, the officer gave them both back their IDs.

"I pulled you over for failure to maintain lane. I'll let you go with a warning tonight. My shift is almost over, and I don't feel like doing the paperwork," he said, adjusting his belt. "Y'all be careful, you hear and... Thanks, for your service, sir," the officer said, winking his eye.

"Thank you," Lue replied, with a sigh of relief. He watched the cop as he entered his patrol car through his side mirror, before slowly pulling off.

They were just a mile down the road when Lue heard the sweet snores from Tammy sleeping. Stopping by his parents, he picked up her son, who fell fast asleep after entering the car. Tonight, he'd seen a side of her she never showed. The evil she possessed, disguised under her beauty was nothing less than treacherous. She humiliated him in front of everyone. He felt deceived and misled by the nurturing charm she displayed when they were alone and sober. He frowned at her, as she slept on the passenger side. His rage brewed, thinking about the thorough cussing she gave him earlier.

"Bitch?" he thought, thinking of the way she treated him at the bar, "I'll show her ass who's the bitch!"

Tammy was still snoring when he pulled in her driveway. Lue fetched her keys from her purse and smiled at the sight of the cash stacked neatly in it. He took her sound asleep son to his room. After several attempts to wake her, he gave up and lifted her in his arms, leaving the money behind. He carried her in the house, shutting the door, with one foot as he looked in her peaceful brown face.

As he watched her sleep peacefully, he thought, "Stupid bitch." Thinking of all the cruel things he would do to her as he slung her on the couch, letting her unconscious body fall to the sofa. He immediately undressed her, snatching her britches down to her ankles.

"I'll show you!" he thought, shoving his wood in her slightly dry pouch.

"What the fuck you doing?" she mumbled, too impaired to fight his heavy body thrusting upon hers.

"Stop! Stop!" she tried yelling over his handcuffed to her mouth.

"Shut the fuck up, bitch!" he whispered forcefully, panting heavily and striking her on the chin. Her lip instantly swelled, and blood trickled to the sofa. Her eyes were iceberg cold, her teeth were stained in blood as she evilly smiled, then spat blood in his face.

"You fuckin' bitch!" he panted, returning an evil smile of his own before he delivered another striking blow to her temple, knocking her unconscious. Lue forced his way to satisfaction as he stroked her slumbered body while releasing his animosity in her vagina. Buckling his pants, he glared at her in disgust before leaving her partially naked and unconscious.

The following day, Tammy gave herself an early start. Once again, she would be taking her son to live with her mother. She didn't want him around to witness what she was going to do. On her ride home, she felt extremely violated. Her vagina throbbed with pain, and so did the side of her face. She was disappointed in herself. She had gotten too comfortable with her simple life and slipped up! Her money was stolen, and so was her pussy and her pride; she would restore with a cold dish of revenge. Once she returned to her home, she cracked open two brand-new shaving razors removing the thin blades. Then, she taped each end of the blade; one end, she taped a small amount of cotton, and on the other end, she added much more cotton, enough to minimize the cuts to her vagina once she slid it in.

Using her house phone, she called Lue. She didn't show an ounce of bitterness or animosity when he answered. In fact, she boasted how well he'd done whipping her ass and how she was into that type of stuff. She told him she 'didn't think he had it in him being that he was a church boy and all.' She conned him, saying he was exactly what she was looking for, she insisted he kept the money.

She said, "Any man that could beat my ass the way he did deserved every pimpin' dollar she had!" Tammy laid the "Heinz" on thick, and before she knew it, they were making plans to meet later in the night.

Earlier that day, the morning air was muggy. Steam rose from the concrete from the early rain, making the dawn air thick and sticky. Officer Smithy leaned on the side hood of the Crown Vic, with his hands in his pocket. Impatiently waiting for his partner to relay the news from a chick he was banging in the data department. A week free of cigarettes, he frantically chewed on a stick of cool mint Nicotine Gum. He was a middle-aged white man dressed in an attire, unlike your ordinary cop, wearing a three-piece designer suit with cufflinks and gold chains. A lot of his fellow officers envied his style. Most liked him, but more hated him, calling him a loudmouth, flashy, son of a bitch when he wasn't around. A lot of them couldn't stand hearing him boast about the different exotic women he smashed nightly and the constant bragging about the size of his cock.

He made a lot of his colleagues uncomfortable, but he enjoyed the shameful look on their faces. He could tell which one of their wives were sexually unhappy. Some of their lady's unhappiness would sometimes show its miserable face during the department's BBQs just after a few drinks. A few of them would get really flirtatious with him while their husbands glared at them from the far side of the park. Most of the time, they were resulting in an argument or fight. Regardless of how his colleagues felt, his job was secure. He and his partner, Robo, were under the umbrella of the Chief. They were untouchable.

Even after he shot that young black boy a years ago, the Chief gave him his undying support. Even though his original story sounded suspicious in the beginning, the Chief and the Prosecutor helped him construct their own version of the truth and fed it privately to a Grand Jury for a not-guilty verdict.

After using the payphone in the market center, Robo, the more harmonious of the two, stopped to get him and his partner a cup of Joe. He was sure his partner would be pleased with the news the wide-eyed, green chick had given him. They'd been searching for Tammy for over six months. Even the Chief had a sigh of relief after he told him, the records showed she was pulled over in Alabama, earlier that morning. The Mayor was riding everyone's ass, and the Chief was first on the list, which made it ten times worse for them! The longer the hunt for her prolonged, the more paranoid the Mayor became about his career. The fact that she'd been pulled over earlier that morning, the F.B.I. would bloodhound her down within the week. So, the Chief gave direct instructions to bring her back alive and for them to move quickly and silently. Smithy could see the hidden smile in Robo's eyes as he handed him the cup of Joe.

"What the hell did she say, buddy?" Smithy said with excitement, pushing himself off the car to his feet; almost spilling his coffee.

"We found her black ass!" said Robo, exchanging the enthusiasm.

Smithy looked astonished as he opened the door to the car. "You know, you're black, right boy?" he wittily said, taking a sip from his coffee as he swiftly entered the vehicle.

He could never understand why Robo would go out of his way, just to fuck up his own people. 'This had to be from his childhood,' he once thought, until he saw how much he enjoyed just fucking people up! White or black, it's just the blacks and browns got a knee in their neck on a good day. Some were beaten so badly, even jail wasn't an option. White people, he would give a slap on the wrist, and if they were an asshole, he would merely cuff them and take them to jail.

He earned his name Robo, from the turbo speed he displayed when chasing suspects, black ones of course. He was the cornerstone of the department, a real Sam Bo. The love he got from the station made him feel he had to exchange black blood for blue. He watched as the young black man bled profusely on the hot parking lot pavement with no remorse. The whole incident could have been avoided. Had Smithy not lost all his cash in Vegas, things may have been different. Robo listened to Smithy griped and complained about the money he'd lost for most of the morning and figured taking him to their favorite coffee spot might cheer his spirit. He needed his partner to focus and not get drunk from life's woes while they were on the beat.

By the time they arrived at the corner market and finished their coffee, Robo realized his plan didn't have any effects on Smithy. In fact, he wished they had stayed in the precinct. It only took the young man to stare in Smithy's direction before he exploded.

"What the fuck you staring at nigger?" he said. Then the bottom of his eyelids tightened, and his eyes became pitch black with rage.

Attempting to calm his partner down, Robo yelled, "What the fuck are you doing, man! He's just a kid!

Calm down, fool!" he said, slightly laughing, but seeing beforehand that this time it may be more than just the regular beat down.

Ignoring Robo's request to regain his temper, Smithy continued, "I said! What the fuck you staring at nigger?" As he quickly walked towards the teen, with his hand gripped firmly to the butt of his pistol.

Having no idea why the crazed cop chose to single him out, the teen got nervous and started to run.

"Freeze!" he heard before he even had a chance to attempt his escape.

"What the hell did I do? What the fuck do you want with me?" the teen bargained, holding his hands high in the air.

"Drop the gun! Drop the gun!" Smithy yelled, from the top of his lungs, before unloading five shots that would kill the teen instantly.

Holding both his hands over his fresh crew cut, Robo said, gasping for air, "Smithy! Smithy! What the fuck did you do man?"

Smithy stood silent, as stiff as a board as he stared at the young man dead, in front of him. His adrenaline spiked his emotions intensely. So intense, he didn't see his partner in their car recovering his personal sidearm and planting it next to the teen whose body was drenched in his own blood.

Robo clearly understood, he was an Afro American. He hated Smithy had to remind him of it, every chance he got. No matter how much he tried to impress Smithy, he never felt he was his equal, and he silently hated him for it. Ignoring Smithy's black remark, he said, proudly, "I know I'm black, Smithy! But I bleed blue! And don't you forget that!" He slammed the car door and threw his half-empty cup of Joe out the window.

"Can you believe this slick bitch been in Alabama this whole time?" he said, starting the car as he shifted gears. He continued, "The Chief said she's a real eye-popper and we should be careful... She's a slick one."

"Well, if she tries any of that slick shit with me, Ima bury her ass, just like I did the other one," said Smithy, patting his firearm.

"Not this time, partner. We have to bring her back alive. That's the only way we get our cut." Then Robo mumbled, just loud enough for Smithy to hear, "Ala fuckin' Bama!"

"To be frank with you, partner, I don't care where she is! Shit, I need the money, and if she's an eye-popper like the Chief says, I just might give her a farewell present! If you know what I mean?" replied Smithy, smiling, showing the gum clenched between his teeth.

It was late when the officers arrived at Tammy's. They both were speechless, silently admiring her enormous house and the shining red Q 45 that was parked in the front. Robo backed the car in to conceal the government issued tag.

"Shit, she sho is living well, partner," Robo said, opening the door to the black mob tinted Crown Vic.

"Yes, she is. I bet my uncle Bobo's prosthetic leg, a chick like her don't keep money in no bank neither!"

"I'm sure your uncle Bobo won't be too happy if he knew his leg was up for a bet."

"Shit, that crazy son of a bitch might try to fight me with it!"

They both chuckled, as Robo rang the doorbell.

"Give me a sec!!!" Tammy yelled, deviously cheerful. Once she answered the door, she left both cops speechless. Her lingerie slightly hid her breast. Her skin glowed from the candlesticks burning behind her. Her thighs were thick but fit. The silky lingerie only complemented her dashing figure. For a slight second, both men forgot what they were there for, hypnotized by her goddess-like features. That changed when they observed fear invading her facial features. A hard-right hand between Tammy's eyes snapped her nose. She crashed to her backside in the corridor of her house, trying to get to her feet. However, Smithy was quick, jumping on her back, pressing his knee in her spine, as he zip-tied her hands and ankles.

Slightly out of breath, he said panting, "What the hell are you looking at, Robo! Help me get her to the couch!"

Her poor body was weak. Her feet drug across the floor as they carried her to the living room, throwing her on the same sofa she was just raped on the night prior. Brandishing his police-issued Glock 45,' he tapped her on the forehead twice with the barrel.

"Expecting someone tonight, sweetheart?" Smithy asked, smacking on chewing gum with a perverted grim smile.

He rubbed the barrel of the pistol up and down the side of her bloody face, turning his head to his partner, he said, "Look here, Robo! We got ourselves a tough one! Now apparently she wants to exercise her right to remain silent. Do you think that's a good idea, Robo?"

Without responding, Robo smiled coldly, glaring at Tammy.

"See, my partner here doesn't think that would be such a good idea." "But," he said, lifting his gun in the air, "Being the awesome guy I am, I'm going to give you two choices. Option one; you can speak now, or option two; you can forever hold your peace!" "Where's the fucking money, bitch!?" demanded Smithy, smacking her fragile and bruised face with the butt of his pistol.

Blood splattered along her front teeth, over the once creamed sofa. Tammy could barely open her eyes. Dark, purple, puffy rings barricaded her vision. A tear rolled down her cheek mixing with the dry blood that leaked from her nose. She remained tight-lipped and silent. She refused to let them break her. Glaring at her sweet skin, Smithy holstered his gun.

"You know what? I got something for you, girly!" he said, smiling, as he undid his belt buckle.

"Robo!" he commanded, "go find that money. I'm going to stay here and make sure our girly don't escape."

"I'm on it, partner," Robo responded before disappearing upstairs.

"So, you think you tough, huh?" said Smithy, licking his lips. "I got something for you, tough girl," as he kissed her on the breast.

Tammy's heart fluttered in joy. She thought of the look he would give her after shoving his staff in her booby trap. Internally, she laughed out loud, as he took her breast, and viciously kissed her nipple. She laid still. She didn't fight or resist him. She let him shove and cuss her without a whisper, not even a solitary word. 'It would be all worth her grand finale,' she thought, feeling his nature starting to harden on her leg. She knew it wouldn't belong.

Once Smithy felt ready, he whipped out his staff and gave Tammy a hard thrust! His eyes rolled to the back of his skull! His mouth opened, but the pain did not allow him to scream. The razors stuffed in Tammy's crouch split his penis clean, in half. Blood poured from her vagina as if she were having a miscarriage. The excruciating pain from the razors sent Smithy's body into shock! He passed out, tumbling off her onto the floor.

She quickly sprang into action by rolling off the sofa and into his puddle of blood that covered her hardwood floors. She frantically searched for the gun he'd placed in his shoulder holster. With her hands zip-tied behind her back, she swiftly threw her legs over the restraints, making it easier to use Smithy's weapon.

"Help! Help me!" Smithy painfully groaned.

Retrieving his pistol from its holster, she found it difficult to put a bullet in the chamber, due to the restraints limiting her hand movements. She held the butt of the gun tightly as she violently beat in the face of the crooked cop. Blood particles splattered on her cheek and forehead with each hateful strike.

"What the fuck?" Robo uttered, reentering the room just in time to see Tammy on her knees, re-killing his partner's corpse. In one swift motion, he grabbed the gun from her hands and with the butt of his pistol, he knocked her unconsciously to the bloody floor.

Robo stared at Smithy's blood-soaked body curled on the floor and chuckled, "You stupid, son of a bitch!"

He continued searching for the cash until he hit the jackpot. "Ole Smithy was right," he smiled, "She didn't keep her money in the bank after all."

He wrapped Tammy thoroughly in duct tape, making sure she was unlikely to escape. Then he went outside and parked the Crown Vic in the triple door garage. He didn't know how, but she'd just done a number on his partner. So, he took proper precautions to make sure the same didn't happen to him. First, he put Smithy in the trunk. Then, he laid Tammy next to him.

The iron table was uncomfortably cold against Tammy's back. Her arms and legs were restrained to the bars attached to the side of the table. Once she awoke, she felt dazed, and her head throbbed in pain. She heard the crackling sound from the furnace as Smithy's bones sizzled from the blazing fire. Her swollen purple, black eyes barely opened as she scanned the blurry, dim-lit room. Fear tugged at her heart at the sight of Dr. Williams in his see-through apron. His scalpels were neatly lined in his apron's pocket. The tools on the table behind him were clean as if they were never used. Roper, Mayor Ford, and Robo joined him, standing over her. She refused to give them the satisfaction of seeing her plead for her life. She heard the four guys rummaging around, laughing and joking about Smithy's misfortune. Then a bright light momentarily blinded her vision. It was the Doctor, showing Tammy the thin blade from the shaving razor, once lodged in her vagina.

He said, "You are one clever lady." Throwing the tiny razor on the metal bed where she could see it.

"That she is Doc," said Robo, shaking his head. "She damn sure did a number on Smithy… poor bastard."

Taking the syringe from his breast pocket, the Doctor tapped Tammy on the arm to find a good vein to put her to sleep for good but was stopped by Mayor Ford.

"No, no, no, Doctor! I want her clever black ass awake!" he demanded.

"Are you sure, Mr. Mayor? It could get pretty messy if I cut into a live artery," said the Doctor, laying the syringe on the table behind him.

"Of course he is, Doc!" Roper said, confidently walking towards Tammy so she could get a good view of him. "I thought we had an understanding, Tammy?" he said, leaning over and scratching his arm, feeling the after effect of the heroin. Peering in her bloodshot eyes, he continued, "You tried to destroy everything closest to me. So, tonight, I will destroy you." He turned his head to catch eye contact with the Doctor and said, "Make it as painful as possible and take your time. We have all night."

"I don't know about you guys, but I don't have all night!" said Robo, "Besides, I've seen enough blood to last a lifetime tonight. Just give me my envelope and I'll be on my way."

The Mayor looked at Roper and nodded, signaling for him to get the cash from the car. Roper nodded back, watching as Robo started to head out the door. He grabbed the syringe from the table behind the doctor and stabbed Robo in the neck, squeezing out the clear liquid substance between his shoulder and neck. He instantly fell to the ground, shaking in convulsions. Dr. Williams and Roper rushed to lift Robo from the floor, then laid him on the table to the foot of Tammy. His body twitched slightly, causing the metal bed to make a thumping sound.

"I am glad that's taken care of," said Mayor Ford, refusing to let Robo out of the Doctor's mansion. He knew too much, plus he outright didn't want to pay him. He'd figured, he'd have the Chief make them martyrs, put their names on plaques and call them 'heroes' for their outstanding performance in the 'line of duty.' He thought about making them the next sound bite on his run for Governor. He would remind people of the officer's lives and indicate he was the only candidate that would make tougher laws to 'protect the blue.' Smiling at the concept, he took a seat in the corner of the basement and prepared himself to enjoy the show.

Tammy's puffy black eyes widened at the sight of the blade's scalpel as the Doctor carefully cut into her torsos. Muffled groans came from the gauze stuffed in her mouth. A single tear fell through her bruised face, as she suffered from the incisions under the scalpel. Blood splashed on Dr. Williams face as he watched her eyes close when he snipped the artery connected to her heart. He carefully removed her heart and liver amongst other organs, and placed them in Bio bags, then put them in a huge deep freezer.

"Damn! Doc, that was some gruesome shit," said Roper as he wiped specks of blood from his face.

"You say gruesome, I say art," said Doctor Williams, closing the deep freezer and preparing for Robo's corpse next.

"I say, shrink," joked the Mayor, removing himself from his seat. He was happy the job was finally done, and he could move past his scandal, without a credible witness.

CHAPTER 16
The Breakthrough

*J*mes laid in his bed, confined to his room. Heroin and depression ate his ambitions and all motivation. The love for football no longer consumed him, whether on TV or in life. The only time he felt any excitement, was when Roper brought him another package. The powerful drug took full control over his life and thoughts. He no longer saw his mother in his dreams, and now he could hardly remember her face. He only felt the hurt of loneliness and the constant urge to sniff brown powder. Forcing himself to roll out of bed, he struggled to the restroom, kicking soda cans and empty potato chip bags to clear his path. He wondered what time Roper would show up with the dope.

His body was starting to itch, and he was feeling the urge for another hit. Flushing the toilet, he heard the doorbell ring and thought, 'right on time.' He threw on clothes he'd been wearing for several days and rushed to answer the door.

"Who is it?" he yelled, running down the stairs hoping it was Roper, with a fix.

"It's Grace!"

The sound of her voice stopped him dead in his tracks. His cravings to get high momentarily disappeared, and he began to value his appearance. He glanced in the mirror on the wall hanging near the door and saw an image he hadn't seen in months, Himself. He smiled in the mirror while checking his teeth. He noticed the spaces in between them were crusty and piss yellow. His eyes wore dark rings around them, and his cheeks fitted his jawbone structure perfectly. Roper often chastised him about his hygiene and feeding his high with a meal. However, his lectures went in one ear and out the other. Feeding his habit trumped food or bathing! Now that Grace was at his front door, he wished he'd listened. He brushed his nappy hair down with the palm of his hand and fixed his bushy goatee. He opened the door, dropping his eyes in shame to the beautiful woman who stood in front of him. That very moment he wondered how he had let his life spiral down so rapidly over the last few years. He went from having the world at his fingertip to a lonely house with a car and a coach that fed him dope.

When he finally built the nerve to look Grace in her eyes, his heart dropped along with her arms, she had open to embrace him. Disappointment and despair were what he read in her eyes. She glared at him the same way he once did his mother. He was crushed for all of ten seconds! He wished she would just leave, and Roper would hurry up with the dope, so he could get high and forget about this moment.

Grace stood in disbelief at the sight of her friend. Her heartache caused her to frown. She held bags of food in each hand. She'd planned to cook for him, but his appearance wouldn't let her step a foot in his house. He tried cracking the door behind him as he stepped outdoors, but the foul odor seeping through, combined with his bad hygiene, made it impossible for her to breath. 'What happened to him?' she thought. Still frowning, she was tempted to cover her nose but didn't want to embarrass him.

"James, what in God's name happened to you?!" she screeched.

Holding out his arms, not for a hug, but in search of an explanation, James stood speechless, deprived for words. Grace's eyes brewed, but she didn't drop a tear. Figuring he would only lie, she turned her back and walked away. James closed his door without a single regret of letting the love of his life getaway. He wondered where Roper was because he needed his fix. His body itched, brain tweaked, and Roper was late!

Grace threw the bags of food in the backseat. Her heart was lost! 'How could James do this to himself,' she thought. She knew how awful his mother treated him. Her mind wanted to let go, but her heart couldn't.

"Fucking junkie!" she thought, slamming the door to her car. She then remembered the scripture she gave him a while back and knew she couldn't turn her back on him, in his time of need. After igniting the ignition, she turned her car off. She couldn't do it. She couldn't leave him. Her love for him was more than an addiction. She felt he was calling for help. Every family member he knew had died, and there was no life left in him. It was her 'mission and her calling,' to "save" him, she thought. There was no way she was going to let the devil win today! She'd known James most of her life. Her father treated him as a son. He had told her Roper was up to no good, and he didn't trust his reasons for giving James such lavish gifts. He knew it was bait; a hook, a setup. He felt it was a trap to sucker James into a life of destruction, just like he did his nephew. So her father figured he would use Grace, as a last result. Hoping James would listen to her before it was too late. If she left now, she wouldn't only be letting him down, but her father as well. She shut the car door and returned to his house with every intention of making him leave with her. She would give him a choice; life or death, and she prayed he'd make the right decision. After several knocks, he finally opened.

"What the hell's wrong with you, man!" said Grace with her hands on her widened hips. "What kind of drugs you on?" she asked, pushing him out the way, entering his home.

"What drugs?! What the fuck are you talking about, Grace?"

He watched as she walked upstairs and entered the living room.

"Boy, you look and smell like a crack head, don't play me!" she sassily said, turning around at the top of the stairs. He was hurt by her statement, and the fact that he had indeed become a junkie; the lowest of the low, the scum of the earth. He became exactly what he hated - Henry and his mother.

"Grace, I love you, and you know that!" said James, sincere in every way from his high pitch voice to his facial features displaying his sympathy when he spoke. "But you are really starting to piss me off! You tripping! Ain't nobody on no drugs. I think its best you leave," he said, staring towards the door. He hoped Roper would knock any second and save him from the bullshit speech like the one her father gave him.

Grace rolled her eyes and ignored him as she stared around the house in disarray. Small pink bags filled the ashtray, along with a few joints. The living room and the kitchen were filthy, with dishes and trash. The house smelled of musk, and she couldn't help but think it resembled him; a filthy house, with a treacherous past. She knew it would take her to clean him and the house.

"Look at you, James! You need help, man! You're not the boy I once knew. You letting this shit kill you! Please, let me help!" she said, refusing to leave.

"I don't need your help!" said James, scratching his face.

"James, do you remember the scripture I quoted the night of your family's death?" she asked.

Boggled by the question, James replied, "No."

James met her at the top of the stairs, Grace took James by the hand and began to quote scriptures to him. She convinced him to take a shower while she cleaned his house. After thoroughly cleaning his kitchen, she cooked them both a meal. As she finished preparing the table, she noticed James was taking longer than expected. She called out for him, but there was no answer. She called again, there was still, no answer. She ran to the room only to find James laying on the bedroom floor with his eyes open! Nearly panicking, she courageously jumped straight into action and checked his pulse. There still a faint beat. She thanked God out loud and then rushed to the living room to call 911.

After years of lying and denying the allegations brought against him by the press, Mayor Ford, through deception and blackmail, cleared a path for himself while running for Governor. He used the media that bashed his name, to spread the news of contributions he'd made to the great city of Columbia. He gave himself the title, 'Mayor of Principle, Family, and Values.' He mentioned Smithy and Robo, making a promise to bring their killer to justice and to make Columbia's streets safe again. The media ate the story up, and he'd finally regained support from the people again.

For Roper, it was business as usual, but instead of using street kids to move his product, he used a couple of cops. He figured things would be smoother that way. He knew their backgrounds and social status. They were decorated cops who knew how to put on a façade for the public. It was as if Ford passed down the torch and gave him the keys to the mansion. He developed his own rapport with public officials in high places. Other than a few kickbacks to Ford every month, he ran the business and was finally the boss.

After finding out his body had gone into cardiac arrest, James decided to clean up his act. It had been years before he touched any smack. He and Grace finally got the life they both once dreamed about with Grace graduating from college with a bachelor's in business management. She, her fiancé named James Jones, and Mo opened several food chains up and down the East Coast. The business was great, and James's life was finally in order. After he survived the excruciating trauma, bitterness, and hate, which he buried underneath his pain, he decided it was time to let go of all things hurtful. The pieces of his life that drowned him in misery had to go.

He never forgot about his mother, brother, and sister or the piece of shit, that sent them to an early grave, Henry. Instead, he tried focusing more on his support system rather than cloaking himself under the darkness of resentment. This was one of the few things he'd learned in rehab. It was the key to unlocking his pain and acquiring true happiness.

Despite his fiancé disagreeing, James decided to visit Roper. It'd been years since they'd seen each other. He was sure that if he wanted to catch up with him, he would be at a Friday night game. Although he was no longer a coach, he found pleasure in watching the kids play football. Besides money and dope, football was one of his few joys in life.

Roper was astonished to see how well James cleaned up. His three-piece suit reflected his professionalism. His timepiece showed his financial help was no longer required. His moves were settled, and he was no longer the starving junkie from a few years ago. Roper felt a brief notion of jealousy, seeing James escape the bondage that held him under so many years ago. But, he knew James was a strong soul and was happy to see him. They talked for hours about the past. He was happy to see his memory had finally returned to him and was excited to hear him and Grace were engaged to be married. There were bigger fish to fry, and he needed James's will power to win.

"James!" he said, as they walked through the parking lot, "I'm sorry for what happened to your kinfolks, but you have to believe me, Son." Staring at James through the dark rings circling his eyes that were starting to puff from lack of sleep he continued, "I had absolutely nothing to do with your family's death. You have to believe me, man. I would never do anything to hurt your family."

James didn't respond, he just stood there; stone-faced, bottling his emotions. He hated Roper bringing up the past when he was focused on the future, but out of respect; he listened anyway.

"Speaking as your former coach and friend, I think it's time you bury the hatchet for good. I have intel of Henry's location. Apparently, he was locked up in Texas for murder. And if you want, true closure, I can help," James heard Roper say.

The mention of Henry's name was a trigger point. Old feelings of rage and despair spiked his heart. His emotions were uncontrollable as he balled his fist. His nails broke the skin in his palm, causing his hands to bleed. All he'd worked for and accomplished no longer mattered. There was only revenge.

ABOUT THE AUTHOR

Sherman T. Smalls was born in 1979 in Columbia, South Carolina and later moved to Walterboro, South Carolina where he lived with his grandmother while his mother pursued her dreams in New York City. She later came back to get him, and they moved to Atlanta, Georgia where he attended school up to the eleventh grade. He was thrown out of school for lack of attendance and fighting. Shortly after, Sherman and his girlfriend, now wife moved in their first apartment at the age of 18. They have two beautiful kids and have been together for 21 years. A Low Country #CityOfSnakes is Sherman T. Smalls' first book but not his last.